More Great Reads from Kari Kilgore

www.KariKilgore.com

Novels:

Until Death

The Dream Thief

Hand Me Downs

Protecting Her Own

The Coffee Bomb and the Corporate Spy

The Great Gold Record Heist

Novellas:

Legacy of the Land

In the Pines

Fantastic Women: A Dark Fantasy Novella Trio

DNA Never Lies

The Box of Possibilities

Murder at the Fabulous Feline Emporium

Team Building Revenge

Dispatches from the Galaxy:

Restricted Species

The Becalmed

Plurapod Pathogen

The Changes Cascade

Near Future Forward (with Jason A. Adams)

Dispatches from the Galaxy: A Space Opera Novella Trio

Dangerous Days on a Pleasure Planet

Storms of Future Past:

Dreaming the Storm

Joining the Storm

Into the Storm

Fighting the Storm

Storms of the Heart

Storms of Future Past Omnibus

Voices Through Time:

Songs in the Mountain

Secrets in the Land

Sorrows in the Earth

Walking the Ghosts

The Odd Society:

Independent by Means of Magic

Protected by Means of Magic

Collections:

Fantastic Shorts: Volume 1

Fantastic Shorts: Volume 2

Fantastic Shorts: Volume 3

Escape into Romance

Stepping Out of Reality

Facing Down Extraordinary

Investigations Beyond Belief

Passages in the Real World

Fantastic Side Trips

A Kaleidoscope of Cat Tales

A Tapestry of Holiday Tales

Aunties Among Us

Four-Legged Heroes

Anthologies *with Jason A. Adams:*

Partners in Romance

Shadows Mountain Deep

Uncommon Holidays

Partnership in Crime

KARI KILGORE

HACKING CYBERCRIME

Dana Sanderson Short Mysteries

Spiral Publishing, Ltd.

Hacking Cybercrime: Dana Sanderson Short Mysteries

Copyright © 2025 by Kari A. Kilgore

All rights reserved

Published 2025 by Spiral Publishing, Ltd.
www.SpiralPublishing.net

Book and cover design copyright © 2025 by Spiral Publishing, Ltd.

Cover art copyright © 2025 by Blackboard373 | depositphotos.com

ISBN-13: 978-1-948890-79-3
Digital ISBN-13: 978-1-63992-064-8
Large Print ISBN-13: 978-1-948890-80-9
Hardcover ISBN-13: 978-1-63992-063-1

Library of Congress Control Number: 2021936153

For women toiling in the IT trenches
Past, present, and future

CONTENTS

NERDY THOUGHTS ABOUT HACKING CYBERCRIME

I've always been fascinated with computers. I know that might not seem like a big deal here in 2021, but I originated in a different century. A different millennium, as a matter of fact.

So even though my memories stretch well back into the 1970s, I always had at least a vague notion that such machines existed.

I've always loved science fiction, too, so my imagination grew up in a world where computers were part of daily life. *Star Trek* caught my attention during its initial syndication run all through my childhood, for example, and I first saw 2001: *A Space Odyssey* in the mid 1970s as well.

Between those two early introductions, I impatiently awaited our current wide selection of talking devices. And I understood right from the start that computers (especially the ones that talk) could be a force for good as well as for...not so good.

I acquired my first version of the magical machine in the first few years of the 1980s, when I asked for and received a TRS-80 computer for Christmas. Now *those* were heady days.

Consider the vast potential of 16 kilobytes of RAM, not to mention speedy and reliable cassette tape storage!

I laugh about that now, with a watch on my wrist with vastly more memory and computing power, but I was enchanted with my little TRS-80. It was incredibly limited, sure.

The important thing was I understood the potential. The promise of what was to come. Storing and sorting things. Modifying the way the teeny little programs I typed in worked as much as I could.

Knowing that was just the beginning, even though none of us could have imagined how quickly things would change, especially in the 1990s and into the new century.

Taking a programming class using Apple II computers pulled me in deeper, and my first experience using a Macintosh way back in the late 1980s felt like a brand new world. The simple—but critical

—advance of seeing what I was doing on the monitor rather than having to extrapolate was incredible.

When it comes to the stories in this collection, that experience with Macs becomes an even brighter signpost along my journey to professional and story-telling nerd.

In the late 1980s, we had a computer lab in college full of Mac Plus computers. The little rectangular ones with the monitor built in and a separate keyboard. I of course got a job working in the lab as soon as I possibly could, and proceeded to teach myself everything about the computers and the hardware.

But then, a good friend of mine named Jason A. Adams whispered an invaluable bit of information into my ear. He revealed (dramatic pause) *The Administrator Password.*

His reason at the time was I'd planned to work summer shifts in the lab, and he and the other admins would be away. College students in summer classes and high school kids participating in summer programs would need help, and yes, they needed to be supervised.

Looking back, I suspect he had other reasons to give me that coveted password, which my job didn't really qualify for, and I technically didn't need.

Especially since we're still together all these many years later.

The other thing it did was awaken my inner hacker, or at the very least, my inner "I wonder what I can do with this information?" personality. I spent that entire summer, when I wasn't wrangling high school kids or helping panicked college kids, learning every single thing I possible could about that old AppleTalk network.

It didn't escape my attention that I *knew* things no one else in the lab did, including the professors. And I could *do* things almost none of my co-workers had even thought of by the time fall classes rolled around that year.

My enthusiasm for knowing how computers and networks functioned continued on into the 1990s, and that showed in the jobs I pursued over the years. From random support jobs with learning opportunities, to a classroom teaching gig that had me studying constantly, to a phone support job handling questions about dozens of applications, to my own days as a network administrator, by then using Windows systems as much as Macs.

That last job in particular had a satisfying dose of being The One Who Knew Things. Who could fix things, and make things work better. And yes, I and my fellow IT colleagues often knew more than the end users would have ever imagined.

Their hard drives and email habits were visible, if you were brave enough to pay attention.

Some of those things I wish I could scrub out of my memory to this day.

It was all those years in the cubicle farms that brought former hacker Dana Sanderson to life in my head. And I'll freely admit I have a wonderful time writing about her exploits from *outside* the IT trenches.

She first appeared when she was still firmly entrenched in an office job, leaning all she could, hoping for the promotion or change that would get her out of there. Her setting in Atlanta is no accident, since Jason and I spent a decade in that wonderful city, both of us honing our computer skills for what turned out to be our eventual escape.

In *The Sound of Murder*, Dana has her own experience with discovering more than she ever imagined about a co-worker. And uncovering a secret that gets far more serious than photos and videos no one should be looking at on the job.

That first story also introduced me to Dana's fabulous best friend Andre Telkin. Andre helps her solve her first case partly because he has a skill she doesn't. A vital skill that arguably crosses into a superpower when it comes to discovering and solving the crime.

Andre returns to Dana's world frequently because he's just so much fun to write. He livens up her world considerably, and he's one of those fantastic characters who does the same for me as a writer.

When I started the second story in this collection, *The Fabulous Feats of Billy*, I didn't know Dana was going to show up at first. I hadn't considered her as a series character.

After all, why would anyone write a series of short stories rather than novels or novellas?

Yes, I do know how silly that is now. As you can tell by the number of short story series I have going on.

The near-future timeline established in *The Sound of Murder* fit the story I wanted to tell in *The Fabulous Feats of Billy* even better. As the stories continue, I appreciate the freedom and imagination that choice allows more and more.

For Glory Lane and the Humid Holiday, Dana heads south to Miami, and the otherworldly setting of a tropical late December. Her teammate on this missing person case is a tough and smart Miami cop who recognizes the advantages of having a brilliant nerd by her side.

The Internet of Things is another of my fascinations, especially looking back at my early exposure to the HAL-9000 computer in 2001: *A Space Odyssey*. That theme of how things are connected—for better or worse—is front and center in *Melting Point*.

The final tale in this collection returns to the IT office space, specifically the unique and strange atmosphere of a big server room. They're cold, and noisy, and often have a bit of a dungeon-like aspect.

Not the sort of place you'd expect to find a cat, and certainly not where you'd expect to discover what this cat drags in.

The fun thing about a short story series is how quickly it can grow. In this case, there are already more Dana stories written, and she has an important role in my novella *DNA Never Lies*.

And I just finished the first story where Andre is the main character, and after having so much fun while writing, I can promise more of those are on the way. Just to give you a fun hint, turns out his stories are going to cross over with *Terminalia*, another short story series of mine.

I hope you enjoyed getting to know Dana and Andre and the whole crew as much as I enjoy writing with them.

For more mystery and crime short stories, along with novellas and novels, pay a visit to www.KariKilgore.com/Mystery. If you enjoy stories from near-future all the way into science fiction, check out www.KariKilgore.com/ScienceFiction.

If you want to keep up with what I'm doing next, get free stories and access to Spiral Publishing exclusive ebooks and print versions not available anywhere else, find out about Kickstarters and other fun projects, and see adorable pet photos, head over to www.ConfidentialAdventureClub.com. Hope to see you there!

And last but certainly not least, thank you for your support of me and my writing. It means the world to me and keeps me coming back to tell the next tale.

www.KariKilgore.com

HACKING CYBERCRIME

KARI KILGORE

AUTHOR OF THE TECH EMPATH AND Y2K

THE SOUND OF MURDER

A Dana Sanderson Short Mystery

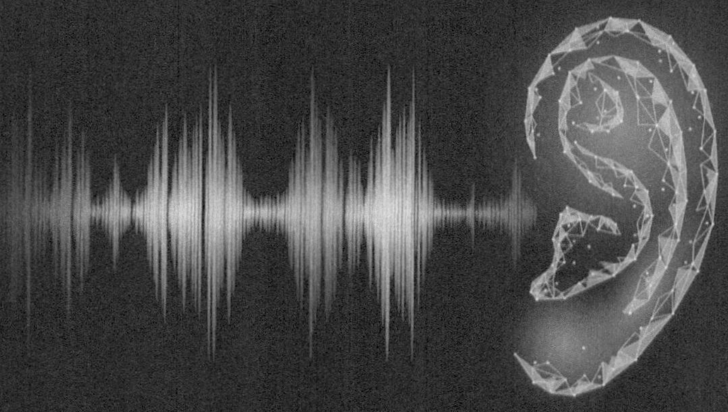

For Audrey

*Who has her own superpowers
and isn't afraid to share them.*

CHAPTER 1

The inhabitants of the vast, pale gray cubicle farm were more restless than usual on an early Friday afternoon. The endless rows of low fabric walls normally created a muffled silence long before five o'clock, neat desks abandoned as soon as possible for weekend freedom.

This week, though, end-of-quarter deadlines loomed over everyone's heads. The prospect of missing their bonus numbers tended to drive the insurance agents and adjusters more than a little bit insane.

Dana Sanderson guarded the calm routines of a programmer more fiercely than usual as muttering, pacing, and understated cursing swirled around her.

The new so-called team-building pods—otherwise known as introvert torture chambers—didn't bother with full-height walls. She had to make do with barely shoulder-height protection on three sides.

As a mid-level code cruncher, Dana knew it would be years before she'd have the simple pleasure of a door she could close. Even if she hunched behind her monitors, the sense of exposure never quite left her.

On the whole, the job was better than most she'd had over the last ten years. The building was in the middle of a typical soulless industrial park, but it was on the CommuShare transit line. When Dana had to drive for some reason, she could plug in to free charging stations. The cafeteria was subsidized and surprisingly good. The huge selection of free holo-training, covering everything from programming languages to online security to financial planning was the best she'd ever seen. Best of all, outside of the four manic times of year, she could work from home at least one day a week.

If only her micro-managing boss would close his own door a little more often, Dana could probably get away with the great sin of listening to her own music. She sat close enough to his office that she would see the gate to his inner sanctuary opening in time to stash her contraband headphones.

Mr. Redmond would never tolerate such a lack of control, though, certainly not during crunch time when he prowled around like a big cat anxious for his feeding. A white noise machine placed carefully between her and the most fidgety of her co-workers helped. A little.

The soft, unobtrusive, and therefore maddening chime broke through Dana's concentration. She would have sworn her workstation had a sensor rigged to go off when she was really focused.

Sure enough, the incoming work request icon flashed red on her second monitor.

Before she could pull up the message, scratching noises against the metal cubicle frame behind her knotted up her already tense shoulders. She spoke without moving.

"Hi, Mr. Redmond."

"Ms. Sanderson. Just sent you a work order. Wanted to make sure you saw it."

Dana stretched her face into a silent scream, then shifted to polite curiosity before she turned around. Her manager wore his usual dark gray suit even on casual Friday, a walking sign of approval for the dreadfully bland office décor.

An odd scent competed with his normal expensive cologne of the month, soft floral notes clashing with assertive spicy musk. At the very least he livened up the stale, recycled office air when he circled by.

"Yes, sir. I have the work request right here."

Mr. Redmond nodded gravely. "It's marked urgent."

"I do see that, yes," Dana said, grasping on to her politeness.

"Let me know if you have any questions."

He walked away, jingling the change in his pockets, surely kept just for that irritating purpose. Not even Dana's grandparents had coins anymore.

"Yes, Mr. Redmond, I do have questions," she said under her breath. "Why do you think I can't check my own work reqs? Why do you scratch instead of knocking? And where do you even get that blasted change to jingle these days?"

She blew air out through her lips, then turned to see what was so vitally important.

Dana was shaking her head before she got through the first paragraph. No, this wasn't her department, not her job at all. Eleven cases, all young and healthy, death benefit claims under dispute. She was a programmer, not an insurance adjustor, no matter who paid her salary at the moment.

Her remarkably annoying manager had not only managed to send the job to the wrong person, he'd followed up before she could even open the silly thing.

She grabbed the mouse to bounce it right back to him, but a flashing note beside the Reject button caught her attention.

Investigation of underlying algorithms required before claims may be processed.

"Can't get out of this one so easily, Dana," she whispered as she picked up the phone. If she had to dig into code written before she was born, she wanted backup from someone who'd been with the company at least that long.

"Jackson here."

"Hey Gayle, Dana here. Listen, I just got a work req that doesn't make any sense. Did you work on the original algorithms for the risk rating tables? The ones for—"

"Yeah, your numbskull manager wouldn't get off my back about that. I'm the one suggested you. Need a fresh pair of eyes. Redmond's sure they don't work. I'm sure they do. Sorry, kid." And she was gone.

Dana snorted and hung up. Her grouchy old mentor was the one throwing her into this particular mess, not offering her a way out. Well, wrong department or not, she was stuck. She skimmed the notes again.

Six men, five women. Eleven marked at the lowest mortality risk, all dying far too young of natural causes over the past month. They lived in different parts of the country and didn't know each other. The only common thread was their life insurance company and their unusual deaths.

She drummed her fingers on the desk, vaguely aware she was contributing to the anxious noise in the office for a change. Dana clicked through to the individual files, but they didn't make any more sense. No evidence of any risky habits or hobbies in the investigation reports.

Only heartbroken families.

This kind of thing was exactly why she hated getting into this side of the business. The code and numbers might frustrate her, but they never depressed her.

She'd do her best, but she secretly hoped the claims held up. Some of them were even younger than her twenty-seven years.

Three hours later, Dana stood and stretched, grimacing when her back and neck crackled. The code wasn't the problem here. Every line was as perfect as Gayle said.

Dana kept her smile to herself as she walked to Mr. Redmond's office, rehearsing under her breath.

Sorry, sir. We have to pay up, and expedite it for

pain and suffering because we delayed in the first place.

The source of her manager's strange smell was clear to Dana's nose sooner than her eyes. The sweetish stink came from a new diffuser gadget sitting on Mr. Redmond's massive glass desk.

He had the overhead lights off, as usual, so only faint sunlight from outside competed with the spherical steam machine's blue glow.

No doubt yet another miracle cure he'd soon try to force onto all of them, just like yoga, meditation, and sunlight bulbs over the past several months. He never seemed to notice he was increasing everyone else's stress by pushing the next sure-fire solution he'd found while desperately trying to reduce his own.

"No, there's something going on here, some risk we're not seeing," Mr. Redmond said when she finished explaining what she'd found, leaning back in his high-backed brown leather chair. Dana wondered how many decent programmer's chairs the company could buy for what that high tech ergonomic miracle cost. "It may be a weird food trend or cure-all supplement they're taking now."

Dana forced herself not to add a snarky comment about the smell.

"I'm not sure what I can do about miracle cures,

sir, long as they're legal. Everything I can see checks out."

"Well, you haven't checked everything. This is a huge pool of claims, Ms. Sanderson. If these pay out, we'll have to recalculate all the damned tables and formulas. No one wants that. I have to be sure everything is on the level. I need you to dig into this, see what you can come up with."

"Beyond looking into the code, I'm not sure what I can do."

Mr. Redmond sat forward and folded his hands on his desk, staring into her eyes.

"I'm not supposed to bring things like this up, but I know about your past, Dana. You're the poster child for turning your life around after a rough start."

Dana stared at her own hands twisting in her lap, willing her face not to turn red. No one was supposed to know about her troubles as a kid, hacking into far too many phones and webcams and online accounts, learning the hard way that it wasn't a game after all. She struggled to keep her voice from shaking.

"If you know about me, you know why I can't get back into hacking, Mr. Redmond. That part of my life is over."

"I'm not asking you to get into their bank accounts. Just find the common thread. Take a look, a *careful* look, and see what you come up with. Don't worry about your usual projects for now. There's a full year's salary bonus for whoever works this out."

"A full..." Dana shook her head, quite certain she'd misunderstood. "You're offering me a year's pay? How could it be worth that?"

She didn't have to do the math. That much money would pay off her college debts and everything else she'd racked up putting her past firmly behind her. The prospect of returning to her hacker life, even temporarily, felt slightly less dreadful now.

"These were all in our lowest risk pool," he said, raising his eyebrows. "Several of them had policies worth ten times your salary. Trust me. It's worth it."

"Is it worth paying for meals while I'm stuck here?" she said, not sure why she was still resisting. "I'm not about to do this on my own computer at home."

"I'll get IT to give you a secure link out, and a laptop to use at your place if you change your mind. Here or there, use your company expense account and feast away. As a matter of fact, we need to keep this one confidential as much as we can until we know what we're dealing with. It'd be best for everyone if you wouldn't mind working from home."

Dana got to her feet. The chance to work at home for as long as this took, away from the glaring lights, constant mutter of other people—and Redmond's maddening scratching—finally met her selling point. Even more than the money did.

"Okay. Have them set it up and give me the laptop. I'll start Monday."

CHAPTER 2

Once she got over her irritation at having to postpone her escape from the office while IT configured her home access, Dana was pleased and only a little horrified at how easily hacking came back to her. She was plainly delighted to work much faster after several years of hunting down bugs in code. By the middle of the day, though, she only knew enough to cause more uncertainty.

The first common thread was a frequent shopping card at Pure Delights, a natural foods chain far too expensive for her own blood. Most of Mr. Redmond's own miracle stress reducers that he insisted everyone in the office simply *must* try had come from the same place. Annoying, but hardly sinister.

She was still missing the essential clue. Time to dig deeper.

Something as simple as archived social media was the first real break she caught. Deleted accounts were far more accessible than most people realized, even after the account holder was eligible for life insurance claims.

Every one of the clients had posted about high levels of stress and anxiety, and their struggles to deal with it were eerily like Mr. Redmond's. That wouldn't have been nearly enough to go on, but all of them mentioned the same meditation program. One they'd heard about on the proudly old-fashioned corkboards by the front door of every Pure Delights store just a few weeks before they died.

Internal Oasis.

Dana knew almost nothing about meditation, despite her manager's best efforts, but she was pretty sure it wasn't fatal.

Nothing on the main sales website seemed unusual, except the option for cloud-based customized recordings, specified to match the client's needs and brain waves. Far-fetched, maybe, but hardly impossible.

She clicked through to the demonstration recordings, then pulled her headphones out of her bottom desk drawer. Part of her wanted to dare Redmond to protest, but he stayed in his office for a change. A woman's voice, tranquil almost to the point of being comatose, spoke into her ears.

"Welcome to your personal sanctuary of peace, calm, and satisfaction. Internal Oasis works with your brain's unique operating system to create the most effective meditation you'll ever find. Let us help you change your life, for the better."

"Has to be subliminal," Dana said under her breath, searching for reviews and fine print about Internal Oasis. A deeply buried company legal filing indeed mentioned subliminal and hypnosis technology.

Part of her wondered if this was a pointless search, driven by her manager's promise of financial reward. It hadn't occurred to her until after she agreed that even though Mr. Redmond didn't say it out loud, he almost certainly meant the year's salary would come with working it out to the company's favor.

She'd found nothing but dead ends so far. She couldn't abandon the single connection she'd unearthed, no matter how vague. A grumpy IT lackey delivering a sleek new black laptop bag, muttering at her to be careful with the damn thing, made up Dana's mind.

Only one person she knew could help with something as tricky as hidden recordings: a life-long friend who analyzed sound for a living.

Andre Telkin answered on the third ring.

"Hey Dana! How's it going?"

"I'm good, Andre. Need your help with a little project here. Definitely on the confidential side."

"Oh, intriguing. I'm all ears!"

Dana laughed. Only a guy deaf from birth would make that joke. Andre's advanced cochlear implant, a nearly invisible microphone that translated sound directly to his brain, was just what she was counting on.

"Meet me at my place in about thirty minutes. I'll bring the pizza and beer."

CHAPTER 3

After four years in what had to be the most boring complex in all of Metro Atlanta, Dana was gradually starting to feel at home. Nothing had changed about the never-ending rows of identical tan brick buildings, or the fleet of last year's trendy e-cars clogging the winding roads every morning and afternoon.

Between a steady income, feeling like an adult at last in her late twenties, and getting more comfortable in her own skin that she'd ever dreamed possible, Dana finally had a clear idea of who she was and how to create that in her own home.

The walls didn't shift from a reclusive teenager's dark primary colors to more girly pastel shades, but she did add coordinating rugs and matching towels in the kitchen and bathrooms. Actual framed photos and paintings replaced the college kid's beat up holo-posters that constantly changed. She'd even been contemplating getting a nicer shifting image display for a bit of variety.

Much as Dana wanted to keep the space as clean as it was neat, she knew she'd have to hire someone to do the dusting and such as soon as she could afford it.

She paced in her tiny home office, watching Andre staring at the brand new laptop Mr. Redmond had surprised her with. Neither her desktop at the office or the clunky laptop she dragged with her for work-at-home days were half as fast as this screamer.

Andre looked just as modern, with yet another pleasing angular arrangement of his kinky black hair, this time featuring a streak of dark red on one side. A thin cable, transparent so she could see the minuscule twisted wires inside, led from the laptop's headphone jack to the magnetic connector behind his left ear.

Her friend's rock solid confidence in himself as a Southern, African-American, deaf, gay man had given Dana a goal to aspire to for more than ten years now. He was the one person still in her life, outside of her family, who knew of her criminal past and how hard she'd worked to leave that behind. She suspected he admired her for all of it.

Andre sat back, disconnecting the cable from his implant.

"I don't hear much in these samples, Dana. Right under the overly soothing music a voice is telling you how the program will solve all your problems, but that's standard sales talk. Common as 'But wait, there's more.' I doubt you could get your hands on anything they've already sent out. Just sign up for the program and see what happens. You could damn sure use a little relaxation."

"A bunch of people ended up dead after their special program," she said, following him into the living room. "That's a little too much relaxation even for me."

Andre leaned back on Dana's dark brown sofa he'd helped her pick out, pulling the longer side of his hair back down. The pea-sized implant matched his brown skin perfectly, but he always did his best to keep it covered.

"Don't get your panties in a bunch," he said. "I want to keep you around as long as the supply of free food and beer holds out." Andre ducked the pillow Dana threw without spilling a drop. "You go get it set up, and I'll listen to them. For one thing, they won't be matched to my brain waves. For another, my magic ear will most likely hear whatever they've got buried under the real thing since I caught the sales pitch. You wouldn't believe the frequency range with this newest model."

Dana tapped her short, dark purple fingernails against her bottle. Andre's plan wasn't any more underhanded than what Mr. Redmond had already asked her to do.

And several hours of searching on her own hadn't exactly turned up an abundance of leads.

"Deal. I'll make an appointment at their office in Midtown tomorrow. Looks like they send them out two or three times a week. You free in the evening for a while?"

"Not free, but reasonable to rent. I'll get you my dinner order by tomorrow afternoon."

CHAPTER 4

On the fourth set of Dana's personalized recordings, the first showing up the same day Internal Oasis' friendly technician mapped her brain waves for three long hours, they hit pay dirt.

Andre turned fast enough to knock a stack of books and papers off the increasingly cluttered desk in her home office.

"Take a little care with the belongings, Telkin!" When she leaned over to pick up the mess, he grabbed her arm.

"Yeah, sure, be glad to. Just as soon as you log into your bank account and transfer a few thousand dollars to a mystery charity."

"What?" Dana whispered. Heat churned in her stomach. "You did *not* just hear that."

"Yes ma'am, I certainly did." Andre fumbled for

one of the notebooks on the floor. "I don't think... You probably shouldn't listen, but let me write this down." He dragged the progress bar in the audio file back, scribbled furiously, then handed the page to Dana.

"This was in the middle of the relaxation speech? 'Your deepest desire for your greatest good is to donate ten percent of your available funds to this worthy charity'? Come on, this is serious."

"You think I'd make that up?" he said, glaring. "I heard it clear as I hear you, right under the smarmy synthesizers. At least dig around in the charity account, D. See where it leads."

His challenging look did a lot more to convince Dana than his words. She closed her company-issued laptop less than ten minutes later.

"They've got it buried under about ten layers of dummy corporations in both directions, but that account goes back to Internal Oasis. This still isn't enough to link them to murder."

He shrugged. "Then we don't confront them yet. Not until we've got the evidence. Gonna have to cough up the cash."

"A tenth of my money?" Dana's voice was loud enough to startle herself. "In case you haven't noticed, I'm not exactly living in luxury here. This isn't the most ethical of corporations. They've probably already been in my bank accounts, so I can't send them fifty bucks and be done with it."

"Well, if this goes nowhere, I'll pay half. But you know as well as I do we're way past coincidence here. If they don't think you're playing along, we'll never know."

"I regret ever getting mixed up in this mess, huge bonus or not." Dana rubbed her eyes. "Move over. Let me log in to my accounts. What the hell, I'll just add it to my expense report."

CHAPTER 5

Two days later, after listening to her seventh personalized mediation, Andre opened another beer and handed a fresh one to Dana.

"Good news and bad news , Dana my dear. At least Ms. Relaxation isn't asking for cash this time."

"What's she asking for, then? The keys to my apartment?"

"Kind of. Just visit this website." He handed her another page covered with his scrawling handwriting. A cryptic web address, jumbled numbers and letters, was circled at the bottom. "You'll feel ever so much better once you provide your savings accounts, credit report data, government account passwords, and any other identifying information you can think of. All your troubles will be a thing of the past."

Dana swallowed half the beer, shaking her head.

"I thought old-school identity theft died out twenty years ago. Seems pretty low tech for neural mapping. Then again, I never suspected it. I never checked criminal reports from this bunch, not once I got past the investigations into their deaths. It might have been in front of us the whole time."

Records like this were probably sealed, especially with everyone dead, but she couldn't leave an end this loose dangling. Andre paced behind her while she searched, a lot like Mr. Redmond would have done. Dana was so caught up in the chase that she could ignore him.

"I'll be damned. Sit still for a minute and listen to me, Andre. We may be into something bigger than we thought. Turns out our meditation clients did file complaints. Financial fraud, petty theft, and yeah, identity theft. None of them were ever resolved."

Her head was spinning with the rapid connections. Hot excitement flooded up from her belly, just like in her bad old days.

"Internal Oasis has more than a million clients," she said. "Even if they only had people roped in through Pure Delights, which I doubt, the haul has to be massive."

Andre's eyes widened, and he got up to pace again.

"Time to turn this in and get you out of danger.

Me too, of course. If they're trying to protect an income stream that big, they're not going to let a couple of amateurs mess it up."

Dana nodded, but she turned away so her friend couldn't see her face. She didn't want him to know the thrill of pursuit had her firmly in its grasp.

She didn't care nearly as much about the bonus Mr. Redmond promised as she did about figuring out what was going on. Finding out what she wasn't supposed to know. What someone had gone to an effort to keep her from finding.

"I'll go in and talk to Redmond tomorrow," she said. "I'm not about to give these jerks my information. Expense account or not, they have more than enough of my money as it is."

CHAPTER 6

Dana walked into a quiet and somber office the next morning, far more so than on an ordinary work day. No one was meeting anyone else's eyes, and several people looked like they'd been crying.

When she walked toward Mr. Redmond's closed door, the hair on the back of her neck stood up. Every instinct she had was shouting at her to get out of there.

Before she could turn around, Mrs. Austin, the Director of Human Resources, walked out of Redmond's office.

"Oh, there you are, Ms. Sanderson. I was going to call you later, but we can do this right now."

Mrs. Austin stepped back inside Mr. Redmond's office and held the door. Dana couldn't think of anything else to do but walk in. The older woman settled herself into that huge leather chair, her gray streaked bun barely touching the bottom of the headrest. She folded her hands under her ample bosom.

The globe diffuser, photographs, books, and everything else of Mr. Redmond's had disappeared.

"Where's Mr. Redmond?" Dana said before she could think of something else.

"Well, that's part of what I need to tell you. Mr. Redmond passed away this weekend. He died in his sleep, apparently of natural causes."

Dana's stomach seemed to fall through the floor. She'd never really liked the guy, but this was too much. Her youthful paranoia, re-born with so much snooping around looking for conspiracies, was on full alert.

Had she somehow put him in Internal Oasis' crosshairs?

"I don't understand," she said, swallowing nothing but air through a bone-dry throat. "He seemed fine last week."

"Yes, it's tragic. No one knows that these things happen unexpectedly better than people in our line of work."

The list of clients Mr. Redmond had asked her to investigate flashed through Dana's mind. They'd all supposedly died of natural causes, too.

"That's what we do, I guess," Dana finally said. "I'm sorry to hear that, Mrs. Austin."

"Yes, of course. That brings me to the next part of what I need to tell you, and it's actually the harder part. We've run an audit of the company expense reports for Mr. Redmond's department over the past few weeks. Normal procedure for a change in management, of course, but your account has shown some distressing irregularities. Combined with Mr. Redmond's notes about your...past, that naturally leaves me no other option."

Dana's heart pounded. "No, wait, I can explain that. The expenses, I mean. That was an investigation Mr. Redmond asked me to do. He authorized the food and everything else. Ms. Steffens should have records of the whole thing, she had to approve it."

"I'll certainly ask Ms. Steffens about it when she returns," Mrs. Austin said with a tight smile. "She's having to cut her overseas trip short because of all of this. But I'm afraid I'm going to have to ask for your keys and credentials, Ms. Sanderson. You know the strict policies about the expense accounts."

"You're firing me? Before you talk to Redmond's boss?" A beat later, Dana's frozen brain finally caught up to the scope of her situation. "My past isn't public record, Mrs. Austin."

"It is most unfortunate that your juvenile record

was in Mr. Redmond's files, but I can't ignore it now that I know. You're not fired. Not yet. Officially this is leave with full pay, as you'll find in our policy. I'll make every effort to resolve the situation, but please understand this is a serious violation. Ordering food after hours here and many times from your apartment is hard to justify, certainly on top of being out of the office so frequently. There's only so much I can do."

Mrs. Austin stood and held out her hand. Dana stared at it for a few seconds, then she handed over her keycard and badge.

"Is it okay if I pack up my desk at least?"

"Under my supervision," Mrs. Austin said, nodding. "Certainly. Any company property must remain, of course."

Dana's mind raced as she walked toward her desk, feet never touching the floor, wondering if any record of her having the secure laptop had been filed outside of IT.

It wasn't like she could get into more trouble at this point, certainly not compared with what happened to former clients of Internal Oasis.

She packed up her few personal belongings, not much more than a couple of photos, her old programming textbooks, and the headphones Mr. Redmond would never tell her not to wear again. She pulled her clunky company laptop out of the drawer, wondering how long before Mrs. Austin realized she hadn't bothered taking it home for weeks. She left it on the desk before she walked away.

Andre was right. This was a bigger mess than any of them imagined.

CHAPTER 7

Dana and Andre walked the exercise track around her apartment complex early that evening, the best way she could think of to soothe her newly born worry about her apartment being bugged.

Every step along the flawlessly manicured gravel track reminded her they were going in circles, avoiding the horror of the investigation only a dead man knew about.

Running a background snoop on Mr. Redmond had seemed like a good idea an hour ago, even with the risk of using her personal computer instead of the company one she didn't quite trust.

Finding his name on a list of recent new stockholders for Internal Oasis only made her fear and paranoia a thousand times worse.

"What do you mean, keep going?" Andre

said, his voice sharp. "Your boss is dead, Dana. Another client of Internal Oasis going six feet under, and a stockholder to boot. You can't keep taking chances like this, and you definitely can't hand over your identity to a bunch of murderers."

Andre had a point, but her need to find the truth was having none of it. She didn't even care about the money anymore.

"Listen to me," she said for at least the fifth time. "I'm not going to give them my information. I'm going to file a report on the transfers out of my bank account. Then if there's something going on, we can report them before there are more dead bodies out there."

Andre stopped, his fists clenched at his sides.

"What if they decide to take hands-on action this time? They might just skip the niceties and send someone over to cut both our throats!"

Dana put a hand on his shoulder, dismayed at how tense he was.

"No, that's not how they do this. Every single person I've dug up has died of what looks like natural causes. No violence, no drugs, no poison that anyone can find. We'll never know unless we do this, and they'll just keep getting away with it. Don't back out on me now, Dre."

He rolled his eyes at the much-hated nickname, but Andre kept walking.

"Fine, but you owe me. They shut down the expense account?"

"First thing this morning. That's what's about to get me fired, remember?"

"Then I'll spring for dinner tonight, you bum. But once you get your severance pay, you're taking me out on the town."

Nearly an hour after she filed the fraud report to her bank, Dana held her breath waiting for the apparently still secret company laptop to get online. The secure connection took a while every time, but she expected sirens and armed guards at any second.

"Wow, I'm surprised that worked," she said, letting out her breath. "HR must not know I have it."

"About time we caught some *good* luck. How long do you think it'll take for Internal Oasis to notice the report to the bank?"

"Good question. They caught my deposits fast enough, or at least they sent out the next recordings right away. What are you buying me for dinner? We've been through every delivery—"

"Hang on," Andre said, leaning toward the monitor. "I'm afraid your stomach's going to have to wait. Your new recording has arrived."

Dana's body ran hot, then cold. For the first time

since this crazy trip started with that odd work order, she felt more than doubtful. Dana was terrified.

She'd probably already lost her job, and at least one more person was dead. Maybe this had gone on long enough.

"We're in over our heads, Andre."

"You noticed. Tell me something I don't know, D."

Their eyes met, and both fell into a mad fit of giggling. Most unbecoming and inappropriate for the situation, and the only possible way to go through with it.

"I guess we can't stop now. Plug in and see what she has to say. If you start to fall asleep on me, I'll knock you silly."

"Too late," Andre said, grinning. "But stand by just in case."

As he'd done since the strange messages started, Andre scribbled the words as he heard them, talking to himself under his breath. This time, Dana sat beside him and watched, tapping her foot.

After almost fifteen minutes, he gasped and turned to her. His face was as close to pale as she'd ever seen it.

"What? What did Ms. Relaxation say?"

"Ms. Relaxation said die." He ran a hand over his face, then took a deep breath. "She counted down again, like she does at the beginning. Relax, feel heavy, drop down into your quiet self, heart rate slowing, the whole works. But after one, under that damn warbling keyboard music, she said your heart will slow to stillness. Your troubles are at an end."

"Are you sure?"

Even after everything else she'd found, everything they'd found together, Dana wasn't ready to believe this.

"Positive."

"You think that would really work? Telling someone's heart to just stop like that?"

Andre shrugged, but his jaw worked like he was trying not to throw up.

"Think about it, Dana. They've already worked out how to get their clients to give up their money, their security, their whole identities. People go to subliminal clinics all the time for weight loss, smoking, drinking, whatever they want a quick fix for. It's not like the bad old days, either. This stuff works. Internal Oasis hasn't exactly been demonstrating the best corporate ethics, have they?"

Dana hugged Andre hard, surprising a grunt out of him.

"You did it, Andre. You figured it out."

"Oh, come on," he said, rolling his eyes. "That's bull, and you know it. I expect my share of any reward money, mind you, or at least a great party, but this was your ballgame. You found the pattern. You kept going when it didn't make sense to anyone else. All I did was lend you my bionic ear."

"I have to hear it."

He swatted her shaking hand when she reached for the speaker to disconnect the cord to his implant.

"No *way*, Dana. Didn't you hear a word I just said? I'll get this analyzed and broken down into the separate tracks tonight, but you know you can't listen to it. There's no coincidence here, not a chance. The day you filed the fraud report, this showed up? I'm willing to bet my savings account and yours too that all the rest of them heard the same thing as soon as they stirred up trouble. Personalized and tuned to their exact brainwaves."

"Gods, we did lead them right to Mr. Redmond," Dana said. She swallowed several times, trying to keep her stomach moving in the right direction.

"He probably did that himself. He put you on the case, remember? Invested in them a month ago, then started poking around in those death claims with no idea where it would end up. I bet we'd find some suspicious transfers out of his bank account if we looked. They didn't go after you until you filed the bank fraud complaint."

"We're talking about murder here, Andre. Murder by meditation."

As soon as the words were out, Dana was again fighting the urge to laugh. She clenched her fists until her hands ached to stop it. This went beyond their normal level of tasteless jokes. Andre only nodded, his features grave.

"You got it. Now we have to make sure everyone knows about it."

CHAPTER 8

Dana's daydreams of great public outcry and uproar never made it past the *what if* stage.

Andre wouldn't tell her where he sent all of the recordings and notes, but less than a week later Internal Oasis quietly went out of business. The industry newsfeeds went silent after a few startled reports.

She'd already hacked into a forum for everyone who'd lost their jobs by the time the founder and CEO, a voiceover actress named Teresa Jeanette, ended up in prison. Nothing there or in the news mentioned the remarkable brain mapping technology.

Dana wondered if that was already in the hands of the government. Or worse.

Former employee gossip ran toward tax evasion

as the cause of the whole thing. No one doubted whatever happened had been hushed up, and fast. Probably at great expense.

Dana and Andre kept the truth to themselves.

The only person Dana didn't leave in the dark was Mrs. Austin. She'd visited her old office the same day Andre turned everything in. She didn't tell her friend she was going, though she did give him credit for the vital part he played.

Sitting in front of the woman who'd fired her, trying not to fidget, sweating, and forcing herself to keep talking when the HR manager clearly didn't believe a word of it was hard enough. Facing Andre when it all came to nothing would be intolerable.

After that horrifying meeting, Dana occupied herself with the long search for another job.

Her first call came from her old one.

"Ms. Sanderson? Bonnie Austin here. I have good news for you."

"About the Internal Oasis investigation?"

"Among other things. I'm also calling to offer you your job back."

Dana had to try several times before her voice functioned.

"You want..." Dana shook her head, trying to force her brain to catch up. "You're asking me to come back?"

"Everyone in management hopes you will, yes." Mrs. Austin paused, then went on in a strained voice. "I do too, of course. Your work exposing the criminal activities of Internal Oasis was outstanding. You're welcome to return to programming, but with your success in a difficult case, we're hoping you'll consider a transfer into our own investigation department."

"Wait, give me a minute to catch up," Dana said. She wished Andre were there to see her grinning like a madwoman. "What happened with those claims? The ones Mr. Redmond asked me to look into?"

"That's part of the good news. Those were all paid in full by Internal Oasis, along with a healthy increase for wrongful death. I'm told many other deaths were linked to them with the same result, including Mr. Redmond's. You saved many more lives, and fortunes, by stopping them."

"I really wish Mr. Redmond were here to see this," Dana said, surprised by a tear rolling down her cheek.

"We all do. He was instrumental in getting the right woman for the job involved by recruiting you. In fact, that brings me to the third bit of good news. Your report to me allowed a further investigation into Mr. Redmond's confidential activities leading up to his tragic demise. Between that and talking to his manager, we were able to verify everything, including the bonus he promised you. You've certainly earned it. The full amount will be deposited by the end of the month. We'd like to offer an equal reward to your friend as well."

"I don't know what to say, Mrs. Austin." Dana was fighting giggles that felt uncontrollable now, and in danger of losing that fight. "I, uh, thank you!"

"Thank you for all your hard work, especially for continuing after our unfortunate misunderstanding. The truth might never have come out otherwise. Take a few days to think it over. I hope to hear from you soon."

Dana ended the call, her hands shaking so badly she had to try three times. She would have given a chunk of the money, perhaps ten percent, to see Mrs. Austin's face when she offered the programmer with a criminal past not only her job back, but a promotion where she'd be paid to *use* that past. Not sneaking around off the record, either, but right out in the open.

No small, ordinary celebration would do for such a bizarre turn of events, and Dana could only think of one person up to the task.

Their long shared history of themed birthday parties, often including sweet, silly costumes complete with tiaras and glitter, provided the perfect inspiration. She managed to connect the call on the first try.

"Andre! Get yourself and your magic ear over here, now! You're about to star in that grownup superhero party of our daydreams!"

KARI KILGORE

AUTHOR OF THE SOUND OF MURDER AND THE TECH EMPATH

THE FABULOUS FEATS OF BILLY

A Dana Sanderson Short Mystery

For everyone who escaped the awful job

And managed to resist temptation
on the way out the door

CHAPTER 1

Billy Jones sat in the middle of a huge party he'd spent the last year of his life working his ass off to make possible, head in his hands, staring red-eyed at his laptop.

All around him, the people he'd spent more hours with than he'd spent asleep loudly toasted their success. The office incubator space that *Fabulous Feats*, LLC, had rented outside of Atlanta still showed signs of all that work and struggle.

Trash cans along the bland beige walls, overflowing with pizza boxes and empty soda bottles. Toothbrushes, deodorant, and bottles of mouthwash decorated overcrowded cubicle desks.

Billy didn't have to pull an inspection to know more than one of his fellow geeks had a pillow and blanket stashed somewhere inside or under the IKEA portable desks or rolling file cabinets. His bare feet rested on his own battered Boy Scout camp sleeping bag.

He wasn't the only one who padded around barefoot or in stocking feet, and the the rent-an-office had absorbed that aroma along with the stink of overcooked coffee. Billy caught an increasingly strong smell of beer as the keg depleted itself, and not always into the plastic red cups brought in for the occasion.

Instead of holding his throbbing head, Billy was tempted to cover his ears. Katie and Deb had made good on their threat to bring in their old-school Eighties boom box, and its ancient, creaky speakers couldn't quite handle the strain of Twenty-teens heavy bass.

Each thump distorted, and the resulting crackle went through Billy's skull like an ice pick.

No one else seemed to notice or to mind. Or maybe they were all too tanked to give a damn. Or too busy celebrating the first successfully funded multimedia tie-in holo-app in crowdfunding history.

They'd rolled the portable furniture aside a couple of hours ago to create an ill-advised dance floor. Eight confirmed and unmistakable nerds, each drinking more alcohol than caffeine for a change. Enough that they were convinced they could suddenly dance in public after decades of carefully avoiding such embarrassment.

With good reason, from what Billy had seen.

Thankfully the glaring overhead lights were off, as usual, and the awkward gyrations took place by the mellow glow of desk lamps. That much Billy was used to, after so many months working so hard in exactly the same soft light.

What Billy was *not* used to, what he'd in fact never experienced one time in his careful, fully planned if dull life, was staring at spreadsheets with a row of red at the bottom.

Spreadsheets that reflected not his personal finances, which would have been nightmarish enough. Billy could have dealt with that by cutting back on cable, movies, going out to eat. Even moving to a new shitty apartment.

But this.

This was different.

This was going to hit everyone in this room, everyone Billy had socialized with for the past year when his other friends dropped out of his life. Not that he had time for other friends. Katie and Deb, he'd known them since they were all in middle school, twenty years and what felt like several lifetimes ago.

This time, Billy had let everyone down,

including himself and a vast list of investors he'd never even known existed until a few days ago.

He jumped when someone yelled directly into his ear.

"Hey there, BillyBean!"

Katie had apparently succumbed to either boombox or beer deafness, judging by the volume of her voice. Her brunette hair bounced in a side pony-tail, another Eighties throwback to go with the boom-box. Billy tried to smile, but he knew he looked more scary than happy at a time like this.

"Hey KatieBean. You really came through with the tunes. I never imagined hearing *Blurred Lines* on an old boombox."

"All the better for geeky bashes like this one, thanks to you! Successfully fledged NerdNest geeks, I might add. Our holo-app is gonna send *The Fabulous Feats of Fiona* into the stratosphere!"

Billy stretched his teeth-baring grin even further. Gods, how his face hurt.

"Yeah, it sure is."

Katie tottered away, squealing when Deb grabbed her and spun her around. Deb's short blonde hair was dyed pink and spiked into a mohawk for the occasion. Billy winced at the idea of spinning boozy bellies, hoping they wouldn't have to add a carpet cleaning fee to this project budget.

Would that really make a big difference at this point, though?

Not being able to deliver on rewards for everyone versus everyone else?

Billy closed his laptop, put his head down on the rented desk, and closed his eyes.

Hell, the keg was paid for, out of his own pocket. Maybe he should go shove his aching head inside for a while.

Not to drink.

To drown.

CHAPTER 2

Hours later, Billy wandered around the empty rent-an-office, stepping over all the plastic cups and paper plates and other mess his celebrating friends had left behind. He'd usually pick it up to keep himself busy, even at six in the morning when everyone else was hung over and not due until nine the next morning in any case.

But this mess paled in comparison to the real mess he was eyes-deep in.

Less than a week ago, four *days* ago, everything had seemed so perfect. Billy should have known then that anything that went so easily as their NerdNest campaign was doomed to not only fail, but to cause bigger trouble than it ever could have solved.

He detoured around a drift of confetti—probably made from shredded coding notes—shaking his head.

No, their holo-app project *hadn't* failed, far from it, though he wished with every bone in his body that it had. In fact, Billy wished it had failed in spectacular fashion.

They'd ended with close to $25,000 in pledges. With the newish and oh so cute and clever NerdNest platform (*People Will Pledge til Your Project Can Fledge!*), they would have gotten at least some of the funding if they'd reached fifty percent of their $8,000 goal.

And fifty percent of a gigantic copyright disaster was still one hundred percent screwed.

The hell of it was Billy *had* wondered about what they were doing, creating a holographic app that integrated parts of an indie book, that spawned an indie game, that spawned an indie movie, that included indie music.

Bits and pieces of all of them had found their way into the app by the end.

He'd asked, once, but he'd never looked into it himself. He'd trusted the easy answer, the answer he was *hoping* for, and continued on in his blissful ignorance.

Billy sat heavily in his rented chair, grabbing the edge of the desk to keep from rolling backwards.

How was he ever going to tell Katie she'd made such a huge mistake, misjudgment, miscalculation?

Mainly because he'd never bothered to follow up even though he was the project manager? No matter how he tried to word it, the end result was the same.

"Oh, you didn't realize you were going to not only going to mess up the whole campaign we all worked so hard for, but possibly bankrupt all of us in the process? Well, yeah, that's what happened, hon."

As it turned out, Katie's confident certainty that they could totally use anything they wanted from *In Her Mage-isty's Name: The Fabulous Feats of Fiona*, as long as they changed it in some way, was pure bullshit.

That would have been bad enough.

Then the book, movie, game, music scores, and everything else were all bought up by a Hollywood movie studio less than a week ago.

Bring on the herds of lawyers.

Every one of them stomping around in the middle of Billy's brain.

Billy tilted his head from one side to the other, trying to get his tense neck muscles to relax. Instead his gaze landed on the mug full of pens on his temporary desk. Several of the pens and the mug itself came from the same, lame place.

The mind-numbing job he'd been so desperate to get away from that he'd landed himself in the middle of this nightmare.

Gossalor Insurance Group.

He picked up a pen, clicking the business end in and out, in and out, staring into space.

What a rotten place *that* had been. Talk about useless management, even compared to Billy's current disaster. And Billy busting his ass doing enough work for at least five people for less than the pay one deserved.

Keeping up with servers, backups, installing databases. Handing laptops out like candy to whoever the higher-ups thought needed one that week, never caring whether they came back broken or corrupted or at all.

Hell, Billy had one himself that no one had ever...

"No," he said into the silent, dark, smelly room. "Forget it. Shut that shit out of your mind, Billy Boy, unless you want to be picking out curtains for your prison cell."

But he got back to his feet, shaking his arms and shoulders out as he walked over to one of the windows. The sun was barely rising over the distant buildings of downtown Atlanta, heavy gray clouds shifting to the faintest shade of pink.

That laptop, it had access to every system he'd ever touched at Gossalor. All his credentials to log him in, too. No way that incompetent twerp

McGranville who'd taken over would have managed to change everything.

McGranville probably never even realized he should.

"You're crazy to even *think* about this," he whispered.

$27,843.

That was what their little startup owed for the initial licensing fees, and that was only to the indie producers of the material. Before the Big Hollywood Studio Accountants even got their own adding machines out and started digging for blood, and Billy was somehow certain they would.

He suspected those accountants, or maybe the lawyers, had been the ones to point out the trouble to the indie producers in the first place, but not *before* the damn campaign funded.

The better to gouge him and everyone else with once it was all said and done. And with their holo-app creating such fantastic advance publicity for a big movie project coming along, Billy was certain offering to kill the whole thing somehow wouldn't work, either.

The only pitiful option he'd even heard a whispered rumor of was the Big Hollywood Studio taking over the whole app project, but only for covering all the fees. Billy *knew* he and his friends would get nothing for a year of their lives. Not a damn penny.

Back to nearly twenty-eight thousand dollars, when he and everyone else had been living and working off savings for that whole year. And on top of all the rewards they were now bound to pay out to supporters.

They'd watch nearly triple their original goal evaporate in fees and still owe more.

The holo-app reward was easy enough, though Billy didn't love the idea of giving it out to nearly a thousand people at half price.

But the holo-phone cases and the keychains and the shirts and the hats and the coins and the playing cards and the bookmarks and...and...and...

That stuff would have all hurt even before the Great Licensing Fee Disaster. The indie producers needed those fees and contracts in hand to clear everything for Big Hollywood Studio, who'd set their own deadline of thirty days.

And of course NerdNest now wanted to verify Billy and company held the necessary rights before they'd fund the project, all within two weeks. Then they'd finally get paid two weeks after that.

Maybe they'd get paid. If only he could...what?

Billy rubbed his face, squeezing his temples.

He likely still had access to all of Gossalor Insurance Group's financial data, and all the programming code that produced that data. And the records of where the money went, and why. He sincerely doubted McGranville would have figured a quarter of it out by now, if that much.

Billy hadn't exactly been a helpful mentor when he gave notice and walked the same day.

He made another circuit through the office, this time picking up garbage as he went. Back at his desk, he unlocked the bottom drawer of his rolling cabinet.

There it was, untouched since the day they'd rented the space. There was even a tiny metal asset tag on the corner of the shiny black surface. *Property of Gossalor Insurance,* and a series of numbers that apparently no one had noticed was missing from that cubicle farm he'd so hated, even after a year.

Billy pulled the power cord out, running it idly through his fingers.

The horrible asset tracking and security wasn't the only thing he knew about Gossalor.

He knew the yearly, quarterly, and monthly profit numbers for the place. They were nowhere near AllState or State Farm numbers, no.

But they were easily a thousand times more profitable than the amount Billy was pulling his hair out over.

And twenty-eight thousand wasn't much, not really. Not compared to the settlements Gossalor paid out every single day. *Many* times a day. Paying out was part of doing business for them, and they clearly had plenty to spare.

Billy plugged the laptop in, half smiling when the blue charging light came on.

In fact, right before he'd quit, Gossalor Insurance had won a settlement with some scammy hypnosis outfit, hadn't they? Internal...something.

"Internal Oasis," he said, loud enough to startle himself.

If he remembered correctly—and he always did—Gossalor had not only avoided paying out millions in death claims for that little debacle. They'd also been awarded that much and more, driving Internal Oasis out of business and only feathering the gigantic, cushy Gossalor Insurance Group nest even more.

Billy glanced up at one of the "NerdNest Fledgling Campaign!!!" banners Katie and Deb had hung all around the place.

He couldn't break Katie's heart, and Deb's, and everyone else's.

As far as they knew, the campaign *had* been a success.

And the product launch would be, too.

Sometimes a gold-plated nest could do without a feather or two.

Especially if no one would ever be the wiser.

CHAPTER 3

Dana Sanderson took a deep breath, made sure a relatively friendly smile was firmly on her face, and pushed open the door to the IT department at Gossalor Insurance Group. Just as she expected even after a year away from this part of her old office, not a thing had changed.

The same barely there lighting, with all the glaring overhead fluorescent lights turned off. Not quite enough desk lamps combined with the ghostly blue and green monitor glow to illuminate the compact warren of dark gray cubicles.

The same freezing cold and painfully dry air, surely more than required to keep any number of servers from overheating.

The same clash of different music coming from two, no, three different areas.

Dana's uncharitable side (which enjoyed working from home and traveling more than even she realized) was half convinced that she smelled the same stale pizza and strong coffee from the last time she'd ventured in here.

The tile floor felt echoing under her feet somehow, not quite anchored down. As a former code cruncher for Gossalor, she'd known enough people who hung out down here to understand the raised flooring for easier cable runs. Same with the lowered white squares of ceiling tiles close overhead.

And she still felt like she never quite got attached to solid ground when she walked through.

She shifted the strap of the black laptop bag higher on her shoulder and moved deeper into the den. Dana had to snort back laughter when one head popped up over the cube wall, then another.

"That you, Sanderson?" a woman's voice called.

"That's me. What are you doing down here, Gayle?"

A rail-thin woman who towered a full head over Dana emerged from the shadows. Dana's long-time mentor had short steel gray hair, matching metal-framed glasses, and a bit of a perpetual scowl.

She was one of the few people around this place Dana actually missed.

Gayle lowered her voice and stepped close to Dana.

"Eh, this latest fuzzy cheeked kid in charge is even worse than Jones was. Busted up my databases five times in the last six months. I've been down here for a couple of weeks moving everything onto new servers, away from McGranville's eager little fingers."

Before Dana could respond, McGranville himself appeared from around the opposite corner. His round face was open and friendly where Gayle's was closed and grouchy, and he grinned as if he and Dana had been the very best of friends until she switched from mid-level coder to special investigator.

She wasn't sure they'd ever spoken more than ten words.

"Hey there, Dana, great to see you again! How's it going out there in the wilds of insurance fraud?"

"Going just fine, Will. More travel than I'd like lately, but it keeps me from getting bored. Plays hell with the equipment, though."

She held out the laptop bag, making sure to keep the scuffed side toward her for some silly reason.

"Well, yeah, you've had this one for quite a while, huh? Time for an upgrade for sure, especially with what all you've done for old GIG. Saved this place a mint and then some. I've got your new machine set up back here, just need to copy your data over, won't take long at all."

He grabbed the bag and disappeared around the corner, still chattering happily to himself.

Dana and Gayle both rolled their eyes, though Dana was alone in having to fight off laughter.

"See what I'm up against?" Gayle said. "We get Jones's mopey ass out of here and end up with Peppy McSqueaky. Sure you don't want to come back?"

"That kind of talk will get me out the door without the new laptop. I wouldn't be here at all if it weren't for that."

Gayle shook her head, running one hand through her already rumpled hair.

"Hell, you could have kept it and walked out of here with five or six more before anyone would notice. Bet it won't surprise you to hear that rig was never even checked out to you. Jones didn't bother writing it down, anywhere. He was halfway out the door by then and stopped doing much of anything. Wouldn't surprise me if he didn't lug a bunch of equipment out of here himself."

"They wipe all those logins, though. Right? All those outdated credentials. Please tell me they do at least that much."

Gayle snorted, shaking her head.

"I don't think it's ever crossed this kid's mind that

he *could* do that, much less that he should. Don't get me wrong, McGranville's not a bad kid, or even a dumb one. He's just spectacularly unqualified for this job and Jones never bothered to train him. One example in case you don't believe me. Your old boss, Redmond? I found all of his access still intact just yesterday."

"Redmond? As in dead for a *year* Redmond?"

"That's the one. Anyone who knew his logins, or anyone like you who's good enough to hack them, could waltz right in and bring him back to life. Hell of a state of things when we deal with life insurance."

Dana shrugged, trying to rein in her curiosity. That part of her made her damn good at her job when it came to figuring out who might be trying to scam the system. But if she wasn't careful, she'd spend all her time digging into things that didn't matter. Or that she could never solve even if she wanted to.

But she did wonder who all could simply waltz right in.

And what they'd do once they got there.

CHAPTER 4

Billy sat at the head of a long oval table in another room of the business incubator, just a few doors down from their rent-a-space. The table was solid and heavy, oak from the looks of it. The chairs were far more comfortable than the temporary versions they'd gotten used to. This room was set up to be permanent, not constantly changed to something new.

The corner room was bright and sunny with floor to ceiling windows, quite a contrast to the den he and everyone else had been holed up in for a year working on *Fabulous Fiona*. Even the coffee tasted and smelled better, and the fresh fruit and pastries that were part of the rental price were a major upgrade from their usual cheap and nasty fare.

They'd had to pay a bit extra to get this meeting

space for the morning, but Billy wasn't quite as worried about money as he'd been a couple of days ago.

Everyone around the table looked brighter and sunnier, too. Clean and fresh clothes, several long-overdue haircuts. Faces no longer gray with exhaustion or puffy from hangover. Billy's friends positively beaming.

"Congratulations to everybody again," he said, raising his voice enough to silence the babble. "I don't have to remind you we've got a bunch more hard work ahead, but we definitely passed a big hurdle. Now we need to plan for the next steps."

Katie winked. "When do we get all that sweet cash?"

Billy joined in the laughter, hoping his wasn't too loud or manic.

It wouldn't do to mention they were just waiting for someone on Gossalor Insurance Group's big policy list to kick the proverbial bucket. A few some-ones, actually.

"Thirty days from when the campaign ended," he said. "Just like we planned for. We'll need a bit of our outside funding to cover all our costs. That may take a little longer to come in."

Katie scowled, tapping her fingers on the table. She'd pulled her hair back into the Eighties side ponytail, a style Billy truly hoped she'd abandon soon. The bouncy look clashed horribly with her expression.

"A little longer? We've got rewards to get out, some of them with a really tight production schedule."

"How *much* longer?" Deb said from beside Katie. She'd at least shed the mohawk, though the pink tint was just as eye-stabbing. "New tariffs are going to hit some of our materials for the phone cases, and all the new inspections are going to delay everything from overseas. Shipping costs are bad enough. Expedited shipping will eat us alive. We miss those two windows, and our profit margin gets even slimmer."

"You're right." Billy held his hands up. "The most important thing is getting the app ready to hit the market. If we have to delay on a couple of rewards, we will. I don't like it either, but you know as well as I do that Fiona's app is going to sell."

What Billy didn't plan to tell them, not now and not ever, was he'd already committed the proceeds of their NerdNest campaign, nearly twenty-five thousand, to the original indie producers of the book and the game and the movie and the music they'd used for their holo-app.

They'd been all embarrassingly relieved to take

the small loss and wait out the funding window to keep the Big Hollywood Studio deal intact.

Contracts were all signed and properly filed, all for a promise of not coming after Billy and his team for more fees.

But they had not one whisper-thin dime to pay for anything else.

So now Billy had to wait out his delicate and precise and oh so *tiny* modifications to Gossalor's actuary tables and their underlying algorithms. One big policy payout, or a handful of smaller ones would do it.

He just had to play the macabre game of watching and actually hoping for someone to die.

And hoping the big movie deal didn't go public before then.

"Yeah, the app will sell," Katie said, still scowling. "But we're going to have a load of pissed off backers if we're really late on these rewards. And that will *not* be good word of mouth with such a tight-knit bunch of geeks."

"I know, I hear you." Billy was almost sure his smile looked natural. "I'm keeping on top of it. We'll be fine, truly. Let's focus on what we can do to be ready. Where do we stand on testing the app with different phone and tablet platforms?"

As he'd known it would, that constantly stressful

question got everyone distracted. Every new operating system update brought a new headache. One
he was happy to let the whole team get caught up in.

He'd worked very hard to keep his mind off of
whichever random beloved person would die first,
funneling an extremely small percentage of their
death benefit into a blind account that only he'd be
able to access. Hopefully very, *very* soon.

Thinking in terms of a specific, real person didn't
help.

Throughout his long night of snooping through
that old code, Billy had instead concentrated on the
kind of person that would fit the bill and ease his
impending guilt.

An abusive husband. A cold and domineering
grandmother. A wealthy old scrooge who refused to
help their poor but deserving family.

Hell, maybe good karma would send someone in
those grieving families to the fanciful, uplifting, even
motivating tale of *Fabulous Fiona*, all through the
wonders of their delightful holo-app.

Billy leaned back in his far more comfortable
chair, envisioning the smiles of relief on all those sad
faces.

CHAPTER 5

Dana strode back into the IT den only a few days after she'd last been inside, carrying bags of takeout comfort food for herself and Gayle. She'd long ago learned not to giggle at her old mentor's love of pinto beans, cornbread, and cooked cabbage. Dana was just thankful the best source for old-style Southern was still open between her apartment and the Gossalor office.

The lights were as dim as ever, but today only two clashing sources of music floated through the deep freeze dry air. She headed toward the left and Gayle's classic rock rather than Will McGranville's perky light jazz.

Quiet as Dana thought she was walking, Gayle popped up over the cubicle wall when she was still ten feet away.

"About time you got here," Gayle said. "I'm starving to death for food and someone over eighteen to talk to."

"I'm almost certain Will is at least twenty-four. Maybe twenty-five."

Gayle shifted her metal-framed glasses up into her disheveled hair and snorted. She'd kept her work-space extremely neat as usual, with only a few well-cared for and carefully notated technical manuals on the otherwise spotless gray and white speckled desk.

"If that kid is twenty-five I'll eat one of these manuals. He didn't spot you, did he?"

Dana shook her head. "Don't think so. He didn't pop up and I can't hear him chattering his way over here."

"Good. This might not be for his ears, not yet. Sorry to ask you this, but nothing else makes sense." Gayle chewed a mouthful of cabbage and swallowed before she went on. "Have you been in the actuary tables or the algorithms lately, Dana?"

"Lately? You mean since I had to go through your dusty old code with a fine-toothed comb a year ago? Haven't touched a thing, and I didn't change any of the tables then."

Gayle grunted. "Didn't think so. Well, someone has. The modification dates on several of them show as a couple of days ago. I hadn't been in the damn things for more than ten years myself, and no one else has need to. Only reason I caught it is setting up these new servers to keep McGranville from crashing the old ones. Again."

Dana swallowed a big mouthful of beans, which she had to admit were the perfect mix of earthy and salty.

"Why would someone be in there? No change notification from the underwriters?"

"Nope, not a word. That notification would have come to me anyway. Listen, want to take a look yourself? See if you can find any other odd changes in servers I'm not seeing? I know my way around these old databases better than anyone else still drawing breath. But you've always been a lot better at that hacker shit in the outside world than me."

"I don't know if I'm better at anything than you, but I can take a look. Honestly, the idea of all the old ghost logins floating around has been bothering me since you first mentioned it. I might just write up a report for McGranville, help him along a little. I somehow doubt Billy Jones bothered to tell him a thing about what he was supposed to be doing."

CHAPTER 6

The next two weeks were the longest of Billy's life.

Not one single person on the Gossalor death policy rolls either kicked it or had their policy finally pay out. He'd rigged his modifications to the algorithms to siphon off a tiny share in either case, then spit out modified results to anyone who might bother to take a look

No one.

How could *no one* be sick enough or old enough or unlucky enough to stumble over the edge into permanent oblivion?

As the days passed, he hadn't been able to resist the urge to log into Gossalor's systems several times a day to see if some lucky soul had passed on and saved his ass. Since no one had caught his modifications to those creaky old algo tables, Billy was convinced McGranville and everyone else had proved just as incompetent or just lazy as he thought.

Maybe one more change would be worth the risk, then. One more tiny adjustment that slipped the miniscule sum of thirty-five thousand dollars out of one of the standing payout funds, then reverted back to the standard formula.

That fund held over three hundred million bucks for the really big payouts. The ones that weren't happening. No one would miss one ten-thousandth of one percent of that much money.

Maybe just this once...

And still, the demands and pressure of getting *Fabulous Fiona's* holo-app and all those rewards out the door continued to build.

The looming tariff waited to jack up the cost of every phone case. Intensified cargo inspections waited to delay them by weeks, if not months. His lifelong friends slowly gave up asking him about the remaining funding, and now watched him walk by without saying a word.

The atmosphere in their little rent-a-space changed from cozy and collegial to oppressive and prickly, too small for the nine of them to share.

Billy's usual tactic of distracting them with

worries about platform compatibility only made everyone look away and shake their heads.

No one had to say they suspected him of diverting the money somehow, biding his time until he could make a break for it

Billy might have felt better if he weren't guilty of the first.

And dreaming, day and night, of doing the second.

CHAPTER 7

Dana rubbed her dry eyes, then tried once again to tame the crackly, floating bits of her hair. Days on end spent in the IT den weren't doing her general appearance any favors. Neither were hours on end spent staring at the ancient displays of green characters on a black screen.

She'd never thought she could manage to work in such close proximity with anyone besides her best friend Andre, but she and Gayle were managing to coexist nicely. They'd even worked out a schedule alternating Gayle's classic rock with Dana's classical, with only minimal grumbling from the other on their off days.

What Dana wasn't managing was tracking down who had been in the code for the actuary tables.

She'd found the alterations without looking

all that hard. A simple adjustment to the payout calculations, less than half of one percent. But catching where it went on the other side, outside Gossalor's servers, was proving harder than she'd expected. Setting up tracking and alert tracers on all the company's transactions had only proven to be an annoying source of false alarms so far.

Until the code actually executed, until it *did* something, Dana had resigned herself to acting as Gayle's second-in-command on moving and optimizing her databases onto new servers.

Thankfully she enjoyed the work and the company.

Not nearly as much as Andre's energy and flamboyance, and he so far had never tired of telling Dana she was turning into even more of a crusty old curmudgeon, just like Gayle. But the calm and quiet, and even the low level grouchiness, suited Dana just fine.

"You know," Dana said, "there's a new Thai place that delivers. Maybe we could try that today, something besides the usual. I think we could all use a break from the beans and cabbage."

Gayle snorted. "I think what you're noticing there is the results of letting McGranville join us for lunch. His digestive system is clearly too young for the job, just like his brain. Speak of the smelly devil..."

Dana turned in time to hear Will McGranville muttering to himself as he walked toward their side of the den. Dana talked to herself, too, a hazard of constant work with computers.

She hoped she didn't talk where other people could hear her quite as much as he did.

"What do you want now, McGranville?" Gayle grouched before he came into sight.

A grin broke across his round face as he came around the corner.

"I still want to know how you do that, Gayle. I was gonna ask you to take a look at some code on the new backup server, Dana, but it can wait until you deal with your alert there."

Dana stared at him staring at her screen for a second before she caught what he said. She did have a flashing red alert, but the machine's quiet alarm was lost under the Rolling Stones exhorting all of them to *Paint It, Black.*

"Holy shit," she said, grabbing for the mouse. "We *got* it. Remember that transfer to nowhere I told you about, Gayle? It finally fired, and it doesn't match any legit transaction."

Gayle and Will both crowded close beside Dana's shoulders, but for once she didn't care about the lack of personal space. She was too busy verifying the transfer, then launching the trace.

"Someone thought they could get away with siphoning off forty thousand bucks?" Will said. "Out from under our noses?"

"Whoever it is probably didn't expect anyone's nose to be in here, kid," Gayle said. "That payout fund is so big transactions this small barely register unless someone's watching. It's held for the richest policies we write. Nothing as piddly as forty thousand would even move the balance sheet. Got another one red right behind it, Dana."

Dana scrambled to move the trace and alert windows out of the way to see another alert, this one for just under twenty thousand.

"That one's at least part of a legitimate transaction," she said, leaning closer. "A payout just cleared to fraud inspection, less half a percent of what it should be. Our sneaky friend would have run out of luck on that one. Anything tagged with an inspection by me or anyone else gets human eyes on it."

"Got a location for the ghost account?" Gayle said.

"Trace working... Got it!" Dana hit the keys for a printout. "I'll bet all what—sixty thousand?—that this account will be empty by now. Probably set up to jet transfers of less than ten thousand out to several other locations, staying under the feds' radar. But I can see where they're going from this trace."

"Get a name, Dana?" Will said.

Dana switched back to her trace program, and sat back so fast the others had to jump away. None of them said a word for several seconds.

"You seeing this, Gayle?" Dana whispered.

"I'm seeing it. The not-so-dearly departed Mr. Redmond has been conducting some very sneaky business. Now who outside of this room might know enough about computers and Gossalor to rig something like that?"

The three of them stared at each other.

Dana clicked a few more fields and ran one more search before she repeated herself.

"Holy shit."

CHAPTER 8

Billy sat at his temporary desk, in his temporary chair, in the rented office space where he was about to no longer work. He'd been there since five that morning.

Since about an hour after he'd gotten the phone call that finally ended the slow-moving disaster.

All his former friends crowded around him now, holding up their phones with Fiona's holo-app activated in all its glory. A floating and rotating newsfeed hovered just above their hands. Even now, Billy couldn't help noticing how fantastic the text looked, crisp and clear even as the colors changed every few seconds.

They all had every right to be damn proud of what they'd accomplished.

The newsfeed itself worked flawlessly, too.

All eight of them had woken to notice of the Big Hollywood Studio movie deal announced that very morning. And all eight of them were bursting with questions, to say the least.

Billy had gotten his own questions answered that morning, in an arrangement he was still stunned he'd been able to pull off.

Turned out Big Hollywood Studio had no interest in having their expensive production of *In Her Mage-isty's Name: The Fabulous Feats of Fiona* tainted by some desperate app developer's dumbass decisions.

Gossalor Insurance Group wasn't thrilled with the role they'd played going public either.

In return for Billy cooperating quietly, and staying quiet, the studio had agreed to a buyout of the app, including assuming the cost of delivering the rewards.

Most importantly, the studio agreed to keep everyone else on to continue development and updates, and quite likely other projects. Billy's friends were all going to be fine for as long as they wanted to be.

Better than fine, really.

They'd be every bit as fabulous as Fiona.

As for Billy, he'd managed to hold off his next

career move until this impromptu meeting/shouting match was over.

For that much, even though his borrowed time was almost up, he was grateful.

Katie put both fists on his desk, leaning over him, her un-ponytailed hair falling forward over her shoulders. Her eyes were red, but her mouth and forehead were still tense and angry.

"What about *you*, Billy? If we're all about to meet our fancy new project manager and everything is peachy keen, where are you going that you can't tell any of us?"

He wished she'd called him BillyBean, just that one last time.

"I'll be fine. Everything's going to be fine. You're all set for life if you want it, and that's enough for me."

She straightened up and crossed her arms, shaking her head.

He knew then running out of time was the best thing. Katie wouldn't stop asking him until he told her, just like she'd done since they were in middle school together. And Billy was scared to death that if told her or anyone else what was going on, the whole deal might be off.

Much as he'd dreaded hearing from them only yesterday, all he wanted now was for the studio's lawyers to show up and handle everything from here.

He nearly cried at a sharp knock at the door.

Billy got to his feet, only shaking a little.

He had the strangest hollow feeling.

Like a balloon, emptied out and floating loose.

"Okay. You're not going to believe me, but I love you guys. I really do. You knocked it out of the park on this one and you should be damn proud. I am."

He walked as fast as he could to the office door and closed it behind him, as if that would stop anyone from following.

Two women and a man he didn't know waited, one woman in a dark green pantsuit and the other two in blue jeans casual. An attorney and the new project managers, he presumed.

Not his concern.

Not anymore.

They stepped past him, stopping his friends at the door before they all went back inside.

Billy didn't look, too afraid he'd lose it if he looked into Katie or Deb's eyes.

Three more people waited, two in police uniforms.

The third Billy was surprised to recognize, at first.

Then everything clicked into place, and he

closed his eyes and laughed. He was afraid he'd keep laughing for at least the rest of that day.

Probably longer.

Probably a lot longer.

"Billy. Glad you didn't run for it."

"Dana Sanderson, hot shot special investigator. Last thing I did at Gossalor was giving you that damn laptop, did you know that? You're not going to believe me, but I'm glad it's you."

He wiped at his eyes, choking back more laughter, knowing it would return.

"Okay," he said. "Get me out of here."

KARI KILGORE

AUTHOR OF THE SOUND OF MURDER AND THE TECH EMPATH

GLORY LANE AND THE HUMID HOLIDAY

A Dana Sanderson Short Mystery

For those of us who prefer winter

CHAPTER 1

Rich would have sworn the last thirty years of his life never happened. The south Florida night air was warm and perfectly humid even in December, the breeze caressing his face and arms. He'd long ago shed the jacket and button-up shirt he'd worn on the flight, leaving him in a black t-shirt and khakis.

The group of drummers surrounding him looked like a random collection of college kids like he'd been back then. Nothing seemed to link them besides sitting in a loose circle under the palm trees and stars and miles of holiday lights.

Yet the sound they created together drilled into Rich's flesh and bones, effortlessly hijacking the rhythm of his heart.

Holiday lights strung through the palm trees and

over bushes that still held their shiny green leaves had seemed so strange to him as a dumb kid, freshly escaped from the frozen wilds of Ohio. Now that odd combination, along with people strolling the sidewalks of Abrams's Bay mid-December in shorts and Hawaiian shirts, felt like he'd finally found a lost bit of himself.

He turned to the left, struck by the odd creaking of his neck. The fresh air brought in by passing cars had dissipated as the sun went down. Rich couldn't find a breath that wasn't heavy and sweet with drifting clouds of weed.

He cared a lot less than he had an hour ago.

The water bottle he brought to his dry and cracked lips was just as empty as the last several times he'd checked. His mouth felt stuffed full of cotton, his eyes full of grit and sand. That much of his past was just as he remembered.

Rich hadn't touched a joint or anything else once his thirties faded into his forties and now fifties, tired of the way hours and sometimes days got away from him when he did. Tonight he'd purposely sat in the middle of two groups passing expertly rolled joints back and forth until he was brave enough to bring out his own hidden supplies, provided by the agency who'd arranged this little trip down middle-aged memory lane.

After a few rookie mistakes and burned fingertips, he'd managed to get his own tiny bong going nicely.

Sometimes old skills came right back.

On a night when all he wanted was a bit of oblivion, Abrams Bay's decision back in the Sixties to turn a blind eye to the lighter side of youthful indulgence seemed like the best idea Rich had ever heard of. The East Coast version of liberal California down in the middle of the Snowbird Belt.

That same relaxed attitude had lasted through his own college years in the Nineties all the way through to legalization for medicinal purposes a few years ago.

The pavement under his backside wasn't as unforgiving as when he first sat with a grunt and a sigh. Rich knew he'd feel the bruises later, and he was positive his khakis would be much worse for the wear.

He didn't care about any of that right now.

Instead of wondering how much he'd have to pay to borrow some kid's pillow, Rich now concentrated on how much he'd give for just one sip of anything.

Water, beer, Coke, even straight up whiskey.

Didn't matter.

The odd shops lining the broad concrete square were all closed, and several of the clerks had joined the impromptu Christmas party a few hours ago. Rich was surprised by how many shops were the same well into the new millennium. The tattoo parlor, used bookstore, and indie record shop he'd frequented were identical. He couldn't remember what used to be where the biggest medical marijuana dispensary he'd ever seen now stood.

The crop of carry-out food shacks that now filled every crack and crevice made perfect sense, though. They were also closed, not smart with such a huge crowd pounding those lap-sized drums that were so much louder than they looked.

Food shack turned to food truck turned to food cart faster than his floating mind could follow when the unmistakable aroma of cooking onions invaded his nose.

Rich's stomach growled, joining his mouth and throat's chorus for attention. He turned again, wondering if his mind was playing tricks on him. Had he actually seen a food cart setting up shop right behind him, or was that nothing more than wasted wishful thinking?

Not just one, but *three* carts. Rich blinked, still not quite sure he wasn't hallucinating.

The rumors he'd heard about modern weed being substantially stronger than what he'd scrounged up back in the Nineties were absolutely true.

The carts were still there, and while he watched, the doors on all three floated up as if by magic.

The smell of hot food bypassed his nose and even his stomach this time, going straight to his legs.

Everything worked as he managed to stand up without too much grunting or swaying. When he stretched, Rich realized why his ass hadn't been hurting anymore. Every inch of flesh from his lower back to almost his knees was sound asleep.

If he didn't get into motion right now, the pins and needles might send him right back down onto that pavement.

Thankfully Rich's ankles responded better than the rest of him, and he managed to clump away from the circle and the steadily deepening drums. He looked around for a bass drum or a speaker or at least something larger than the bongos all the kids were cradling.

They all looked the same.

The carts were lit from within now, and Rich saw the steam he'd been smelling. Instead of reading the signs, he staggered to the closest one. A waifish blonde girl standing in front of it smiled just as his vision doubled and the drums shook the ground beneath his feet.

Rich widened his eyes as best he could, holding out both hands for the red plastic cup she held.

Without looking at the contents, he swallowed convulsively, drinking all the...apple juice or white wine or flat soda in a few gulps.

He didn't much care what it was.

Rich closed his eyes and knew only oblivion.

CHAPTER 2

Dana Sanderson had always hated being called in on police cases. But at least this one wasn't a bloody mess. She leaned against her car on the civilian side of the row of yellow police tape, iced coffee in hand, watching the uniforms crawl all over the scene.

Abrams Bay never had been her kind of hangout.

Pretty enough, with the palm trees around a modern version of an old-fashioned town square. The sharp-edged bricks on the ground and brand-new wooden fencing took away any impression of age.

None of the weird shops were open at nine in the morning, though, and no one had bothered to clean up the remains of what looked like an early Christmas party the night before. All the same kinds of New Age-ish or just plain weird shops lingered around Little Five Points back in Atlanta, too.

Piercing shops, stores full of goofy looking goth and vintage clothing.

Storefronts full of crystals and little metal pyramids and tarot cards.

Dana hadn't spent much in Little Five, either.

Drifts of soda cans and food wrappers had snagged against the strangely green landscaping, with cigarette butts scattered through almost like snowflakes. Snow she wasn't going to see all the way on the other side of the country from where she'd grown up in Pennsylvania. She'd had a better chance of at least solidly chilly weather up in Atlanta.

Dana lifted her thick brunette ponytail away from her neck, letting the breeze dry the sweat. She wore a t-shirt and jeans, and her constant round metal Ray-bans against the glare.

What she wouldn't give for a simple cloudy day.

She could see cords from Christmas lights running up the trunks of the palm tree decorations in the shop windows. A bunch of her co-workers in the Sun Coast branch of her insurance company had been running around wearing Santa hats, which looked especially silly with their perfect suntans and summer-weight clothes.

But deep in her East Coast soul, she wasn't sure she'd ever believe this was December.

Several of the uniforms were clustered around a narrow alley between a tattoo parlor and a used record store. Dana couldn't see what they were looking at, but one of them waved her arm. Another swarm ran over and started handing out clear plastic evidence bags.

Ugh, maybe it was bloody after all.

She held her breath when a woman wearing suspiciously formal street clothes headed her way. She'd worked with enough detectives in her investigation job with the insurance company to know the type.

A light-weight but dark brown pantsuit, jacket folded carefully over her arm. A little flip notebook in that same hand even in the age of the smartphone.

"Ms. Sanderson?"

"Dana, please."

"Detective Michelle Rodriguez."

Detective Rodriguez had a firm, cool grip, and the heat didn't seem to be bothering her one bit even with a beige fitted shirt. She looked Dana up and down, then took off her own aviators.

"Fair enough. Call me Michelle. They called you in on what, some kind of insurance policy for the victim?"

"I don't know what kind of policy it was, or why I'm here yet. I'm in the investigations department out of Atlanta, out here teaching new cybersecurity procedures to the Sun Coast office."

Michelle nodded, flipping pages in her little notebook.

"Okay, checks out. From what I know, you were called in over a clause in a business insurance policy, but you'll see more of that for yourself now that we have some leads."

Dana shook her head, trying to catch up. She wished for the thousandth time that her best friend and work partner Andre was out here with her. He caught things no one else did, even without his electronically enhanced hearing.

Dana had always been more comfortable with codes and computers than people.

"A lead on who?" she said. "For what? I don't even know the claimant's name."

"We got a missing persons report on a Rich Walters a couple of days ago. His business associates only had a plane ticket to go on. We've had the word out, but he disappeared after he flew into Miami. Not a trace until right here, last night."

Michelle held up one of those evidence bags with a scuffed brown leather wallet inside, with a loose driver's license pressed against the plastic.

Rich Walters, from Columbus, Ohio.

"Okay. Let me copy that name and address down, and I'll have something to go on." Dana glanced at the alley where a few uniforms still lingered, heads down. "He's not... Is he over there?"

Michelle looked over her shoulder, then turned back to Dana with a grin.

"Don't worry, Dana. He's not dead, not that we know of. He was here last night. Several people saw him. But now Rich Walters isn't just missing. He's disappeared into thin air."

CHAPTER 3

Dana closed the door to her glorified hotel room with a sigh, leaning back against the cool metal of the door. *Cool* being the operative word. Eighty degrees and high humidity might not sound like much to her when she was back in Georgia. It got hotter than that by March, and eighty in August could feel like a cold snap.

But going from the mid-forties and raining to sunny and hot in a short flight was a bit much.

She crossed the miniature living room, not a whole lot bigger than her office at work, and stepped into the closet-sized kitchen. Barely enough room for a refrigerator, range, sink, and dishwasher. All nice stuff, though, with a few feet of black granite counters and sedate, stylish lighting.

The whole place was like that, really. Nice materials on the walls and floor, much better furniture and fixtures than Dana had in her own apartment.

And every bit of it was generic corporate hotel forgettable.

Even the holiday decorations were tasteful and non-offensive. Neutral-color ornaments, copper and brass garlands. A selection of three-dimensional snowflakes in wood, aluminum, and brass scattered across the tables.

Data grabbed a carafe full of cold-brew coffee out of the fridge, and added it to a slug of cold chocolate milk. She'd definitely take the cold-brew habit back home with her if nothing else.

Two short steps took her to the desk barely big enough to hold her screamer of a work laptop, a bonus from one of her more spectacular adventures with Andre. That adventure had reacquainted Dana with youthful hacking skills that she'd thought dead and buried, along with her juvenile record.

And now those newly refreshed skills made her a very nice living instead of landing her in jail.

She grinned as she always did when the turn in her fortunes crossed her mind, then got herself logged in.

Sure enough, right at the top of her confidential inbox, marked urgent.

Dana took a sip and started reading.

Rich Walters, fifty-one. He'd been listed as the beneficiary on a business insurance policy, but he'd also been listed as one of the protected parties. Or the business had, rather. A well-funded digital media startup, with Rich listed as Chief Development Officer.

Dana blinked and rubbed her eyes. For that much coverage, the startup had to be extremely well-funded, or with crazy potential.

Old Rich had nearly a ten-million-dollar benefit to his partners.

"It can't be that damn simple," Dana whispered. "Ship him down south and off him? And it takes me all of five minutes to catch them?"

At a soft chime, she switched back to her confidential email. Sure enough, Detective Rodriguez had sent the communications between her precinct and Rich Walters' business partners.

If these folks had offed him on purpose, they deserved all the awards in Hollywood. Not just for acting, but for writing.

Each message was more panicked than the last.

If the good folks of MindInPlay Media, Inc., were to be believed, they'd had no idea he was leaving, much less where he was going or why. He'd vanished without warning barely two weeks before they had a massive product update due to their investors.

But investors in *what?*

Was it worth taking someone out like this, making them disappear?

Dana had uncovered more than one business scheme that led to murder, so she wasn't about to assume the best with this kind of money on the table.

Much as she preferred email, the shelter of calm zeros and ones, it was time to make a few phone calls. She started with MindInPlay's CEO, the main point of contact on the business insurance policy.

A relentlessly cheerful version of *Jingle Bells* assaulted her ears before the call was connected.

"MindInPlay, Daniel Montgomery here."

"Mr. Montgomery, Dana Sanderson here. I'm calling from Gossalor Insurance."

After a long pause and several deep breaths, Mr. Montgomery finally spoke.

"Did...did you find Rich?"

"No, sir. Not yet."

"Oh *thank* you *lord!*"

Dana held the phone back from her ear, equal parts puzzled and wanting to protect her hearing.

"I'm sorry, Ms. Sanderson, I shouldn't have shouted like that. It's just that we've been worried sick about him, and so afraid something awful happened. Well, something awful *did* happen, or he wouldn't just disappear like this, but I mean something *worse*, something no one can fix, since Rich is the one who fixes things, and... I'm sorry."

Dana shook her head. Mr. Montgomery sounded exactly like his emails. He had a flat sort of Midwestern accent, a little bit nasal.

But he worked the volume like a pro.

"I understand this is upsetting. I'm not calling to trigger the policy or anything like that. I just want to get an idea what might have happened."

"I just wish I *knew* what happened. The police called earlier, they found his wallet and one shoe, in some kind of college town? None of that makes sense. He was fifty-one, he *is* fifty-one. Not some kind of silly kid. He's got a family of his own, and we're on the edge of some amazing things here because of him. Why would he *do* this?"

Dana took a long drink of her coffee, wishing she could offer some to Mr. Montgomery. Or maybe he'd be better off with some kind of soothing tea instead.

Dana could easily get into the policy itself, but she might learn more from a human's answer than from cold lines of text.

"We can't know why until *we* know what's happened. Can you give me an idea what you do, sir? Why the policy is such a big one?"

A small gasp came over the line.

"You don't think..."

"No, of course not. It's just a rather large sum for a startup, for one person within the company. That's all."

"That's because of what Rich did. What he's *going* to do. We're going to revolutionize entertainment because of him. MindInPlay isn't just a catchy name. That's what we're doing here. Putting your mind *in* the story. Not feeding the story to your mind."

"You mean virtual reality?"

"Nothing so primitive, no." Mr. Montgomery laughed, and he finally sounded calmer. "Rich worked out how to change the landscape of entertainment. Instead of watching the movie, reading the book, you'll be *living* it. Part of it. That's his genius. He's worth a hell of a lot more than ten million dollars."

Dana sat back, lips pursed in a silent whistle. Now it was starting to make sense, at least form her side.

"No one likes this kind of question, Mr. Montgomery, but what about competitors? Anyone who might be willing to take out your chief development officer? Or kidnap him, maybe?"

"The police already asked all of this, Ms. Sanderson. I can't tell you any more than I told them. What we're doing isn't exactly public knowledge. Unless someone has access to *your* files, no one knows enough to go after Rich. There has to be something else."

The man's tone had gone from panic-stricken to excited to cold and suspicious, all in a few minutes.

"Only one more question, sir, then I'll let you go. I'm afraid it's another sensitive one, but I need to learn all I can. Is it possible Mr. Walters was working with someone else on part of his technology? Someone who might be able to help us find him?"

"No, it is *not* possible. Richard Walters was the founder of MindInPlay Media, and he's been involved in every stage since the beginning. I cannot and will not accept that he's been working behind my back. The man I know would *never* do such a thing at all, and he certainly wouldn't do it right before Christmas. As I've already said, there has to be something else. I suggest *you* go find it."

And the line went dead.

Dana was surprised she didn't see frost on her phone from that last answer.

Well, one more call, and this one might be even more unpleasant.

"Walters residence, this is Regina."

CHAPTER 4

After an even shorter, but not nearly as chilly, conversation, Dana finally had two things she could sink her investigative teeth into. Mrs. Walters believed the same things Mr. Montgomery had, mostly.

Honest, hardworking, not trying to hurt anyone at his company.

But when Dana had told her where Rich Walters' wallet had been found, her voice had taken on a weary, resigned tone.

"Abrams Bay. I should have known. If he was there, one of his absolutely useless college buddies would be involved somehow. The guy you're looking for is Chuck Schoenson. Probably cooking up some fool scheme or another, trying to drag Rich into it. Rich is a smart man, but he gets weak when it comes to Chuck. And Chuck knows it. He won't even leave Rich alone at Christmas."

The other was an email address, not the one registered with MindInPlay or anywhere else. One the two of them had created not long after they'd first met, in a computer lab in college.

Regina Walters sounded like she was about to cry, but she also sounded desperate to get her husband back. Or at least find out what happened to him.

Dana started the deep search for Chuck Schoenson, figuring breaking into the email would be the harder task. Much to her surprise, she got right in.

dh2o_70@richandreg.net went well back into the 2000s, and it was about as unexciting a record of someone's digital life as Dana had ever seen. The usual searches found no secret flirtations, no get rich quick schemes, no hidden criminal activity.

Nothing more than an ordinary guy's correspondence with friends.

The only thing that caught her eye was the name Regina Walters had mentioned. Rich had unfailingly called him Chuckie-boy, but the address line and the underlying information were both a match.

Their last correspondence had been several months ago, though. And nothing more than some old college nostalgia bullshit.

Dana switched over to the search and found the opposite problem. Regina Walters was right.

Chuckie-boy had been involved in pretty much every plot and moneymaking scheme under the sun at one time or another. Time shares, penny stocks, multi-level marketing. You name it, he'd tried it. And he'd left his registered domains scattered for the world to see.

At least people like Dana who knew how to look for them.

She started to dial his latest registered phone number, then stopped, tapping her finger on the touchpad. She'd never known whether to call a moment like this a hunch, instinct, or nothing more than a gut sense.

But Dana had learned to trust them when they came.

She'd followed one out of hacking right before she'd gotten herself into real trouble. And she'd followed another back into legitimate coding, and then into her fantastic new job.

She knew the last thing she needed to do was let this Chuck character know who she was or why she was calling.

Dana switched her phone to encrypted mode.

"Glory Lane Enterprises."

"Hello. My name is Elsie Smith, and I'm interested in your services. May I speak to Mr. Schoenson, please?"

"He's not in right now, but I can try to make an appointment for you. The holidays are our busiest season. May I ask who referred you to us, Ms. Smith?"

Dana thought for a second, then decided to roll the dice.

"Rich Walters did."

She heard muffled voices and rolled her eyes at a company that didn't even have a real hold button.

A rustle, and a cleared throat later...

"Luckily he has an opening on his calendar for this afternoon, ma'am. Two o'clock okay?"

"That's perfect. Give me the address and I'll be there."

As soon as the call ended, Dana switched back to the old email account.

There was that hunch again.

The last two emails were from gle.net. Too close a match to Glory Lane Enterprises to ignore. She ran a quick search on the company, but all she found was a generic page promising tourism like no other.

Like about a thousand pages all over Florida, unfortunately.

The messages were much more interesting. Both mentioned not only Abrams Bay, but the square where Rich Walters had last been seen. She looked back at the address she'd just been given, and ran a quick search.

A chill raced across Dana's flesh that the air conditioning and the coffee couldn't explain.

The address for Glory Lane Enterprises, or at least where she was supposed to meet Chuck Schoenson, was only two blocks away from that square.

If those two things *were* related—and the evidence was really piling up—the last thing she wanted to do was walk right into what was going on.

Her next call was to Detective Michelle Rodriguez.

CHAPTER 5

Detective Rodriguez met Dana back at the last place anyone had last seen Rich Walters, in a much less obvious outfit this time. Now she wore blue knee-length shorts and a flowery tank top. She'd even switched out the aviators for an oversized white pair of sunglasses.

The number of people walking around wearing Santa hats or Santa-themed clothing had gone up dramatically, so Dana suspected standing out wasn't that much of a worry.

The hats in particular amazed her in the muggy afternoon air.

A quick conversation didn't get Dana any more information than she already had, except when it came to Chuck Schoenson. Neither Detective Rodriguez—who still insisted on being called

Michelle—or anyone else on the police force thought highly of him.

He hadn't been in serious legal trouble, not quite.

But he was well-known for skirting the very edge of the law, and people around him often fell right over that edge.

"I'm not so sure you should just walk in there, Dana." Michelle kept glancing toward the meeting place, then down at her watch. "This Glory Lane Enterprises was only established back in October. We found the same thing you did, generic language about unique tourism but not much else. Probably another of Schoenson's shell games. We still don't know what this guy did to Rich Walters, if he did anything at all."

"Well, did any of your searches turn up a place Walters could be? No? Mine didn't either. Unless you want to try to a raid or something, we're going to have to make contact somehow."

Michelle shook her head.

"You should at least be wearing a damn wire."

"Do you have a cell phone on you?" Dana said. She got hers out and waited for Michelle to do the same. "I set mine up so it can keep a call connected, so you'll be able to listen in. Some silly thing I was working on with a friend of mine so we could...

Never mind. I'll open this app, and you put your number in."

Dana watched the atomic fallout warning symbol spinning, another of her little jokes with Andre.

"Now the line is connected. I can lock my phone on, but not recording. If you hear something weird, you come in and get me. If I see something weird, I'll threaten to call the cops. Again, you come get me. Do you know Morse Code?"

"Morse Code? You have got to be kidding me!"

"You learned it at some point, right?" Dana said, smiling. She was about to lose her nerve on this whole insane enterprise.

"Yeah, I know Morse Code. Exactly what I expected to be using with a damn smartphone. Not recording, huh? Should I even ask if this is legal?"

"I honestly have no idea. But it should work for now. We'll figure the rest out later."

CHAPTER 6

The address Glory Lane Enterprises had given Dana turned out to be an ordinary office set into an old brick building. It looked like maybe half the spaces had been cleaned up and were in use, but the rest were dark and dusty.

A glass door painted with holly leaves and candy canes opened on a basic tan reception area that reminded Dana of the get-your-act-together-or-else facilities she'd visited as a teenager.

The ones that had only been a preview of the much larger, much stricter facilities she would have ended up in as an adult if she hadn't turned her life around.

Plain metal desk, beat up wooden chair behind it, two in front. Filing cabinets and a coat rack, and not much else. A rattling miniature refrigerator on the floor. Dana tried not to wrinkle her nose at the stink of a coffee carafe left on the burner too long, too many times.

At least it was cool inside.

A broad, burly man wearing a Hawaiian shirt covered with red sleighs and brown reindeer with matching red noses walked through a door to the left. He looked like he'd been a bodybuilder or maybe a football player years ago, but he'd gone a bit to seed since.

"Mr. Schoenson?" Dana said stepping forward and holding out her hand. "I'm Elsie Smith."

The man didn't shake it.

"Take a seat. You got it, I'm Chuck Schoenson." He sat behind the desk and placed his big, square hands flat on top. "I've known Rich Walters for almost thirty years. He's never mentioned anyone by your name."

"Oh, we work together, back in Columbus. He told me how happy he was with your services, and that if I was ever in town, I should pay you a visit."

"Did he now? When was that?"

Dana looked toward the water-stained ceiling, tapping a finger on her chin.

She hoped Michelle was still listening in.

"Oh, just a couple of weeks ago."

Mr. Schoenson grinned. It was not a friendly or reassuring expression.

"And you came all the way down here from Ohio, right before Christmas? That's just fantastic! I know Rich will be pleased when he sees you. Let me get you something to drink. You have to be burning up down here in this heat."

Still grinning, he leaned over to the noisy refrigerator. He sat back up with a clear glass decanter full of what looked like apple juice and a red plastic cup.

"I always knew I could trust old Rich," he said, pouring the cup full. "He just loves to share good news, but you know that if you work with him. What are you, some kind of security officer?"

"No, not at all. I work in software design."

Dana stared at the cup he held out, then back up at him.

No way in hell was she going to drink whatever that was.

She slipped her hand over the phone in her pocket.

"Software design! Well isn't that wonderful." Mr. Schoenson held out the cup again. "I'm sure Rich would have mentioned you since that's *his* department."

When Dana shook his head, he set it on the desk with a sigh.

Dana tapped her phone through her pocket.

Three quick taps. Three slower ones. Three quick ones again.

SOS.

"That's too bad," Mr. Schoenson said, and he actually managed to sound sad through his now terrifying grin. "The drink's a lot easier."

Dana stood at the same time he did.

The biggest difference was he had a knife.

A big, sharp, ugly one.

"Just sit back down," he said. "Nothing to worry about. We'll go in the back and see Rich, and let him tell us if he knows who the hell you are. If he does, we'll all be fine. If he—"

Dana had never been so glad to feel a blast of warm air against her back in her whole life.

"Stop right there! Detective Rodriguez, Abrams Bay Police! I've got you in my sights, Schoenson. Put the knife down and your hands on the table. Now."

CHAPTER 7

Once they found Rich Walters, groggy but unharmed in another room in the same building, everything fell into place.

Or fell apart, if you asked Chuck Schoenson.

In this case, Rich's wife Regina had the better inside information. Rich's business partner Daniel Montgomery was going to be heartbroken once he knew the whole truth. But at least he'd have his partner back, for better or for worse.

Dana wouldn't have minded watching that confrontation through a hidden camera, maybe, but she was thankful she didn't have to make that phone call.

Now that Rich was alive and well, her part in the case was finished.

Turned out Rich had panicked at the imminent

demonstration of MindInPlay's technology. He was afraid anything less than a spectacular result would sour the whole deal, and the huge amounts of money already poured into their business.

He'd gotten in touch with old Chuckie-boy at exactly the wrong time.

Michelle Rodriguez sat across the tiny kitchen table in Dana's long-term stay apartment the day after the arrest and raid. Only a couple of days until Christmas Eve.

Rather than joining in the holiday clothing mania outside, she was back in her too-obvious pantsuit, and shaking her head with her eyes closed.

"I thought your boy Rich was smarter than that. Falling for the chance to be a tourist in your own past? Some kind of time warp memory lane?"

"*Glory* Lane, not memory," Dana said. "Schoenson had Rich convinced that he had a secret formula that would let him relive the best memories of his past. The weed laced with opium Rich smoked that night was only the beginning. Once he had a swig of Chuck's knockout juice, Rich dropped out of sight."

Michelle took a long drink of water, still shaking her head.

"What was he going to do? Try to ransom Rich back to MindInPlay?"

"That's the best part," Dana said. "And the saddest. Chuck figured if he did Rich down here, he'd be able to talk Rich into cutting Chuck in on the deal. Making him part of MindInPlay and using that to get Glory Lane off the ground. Could have been a great combination if Chuck hadn't been lying through his teeth about the whole thing."

"So now what? Rich goes back with his tail between his legs and they get back to business as usual?"

Dana laughed. "It's his technology, so I guess they have to take him back. His wife already did, but she's over the moon that Chuckie-boy is finally locked up. I somehow doubt his business partners will be quite so forgiving."

Michelle stared up at the ceiling for a few seconds, then looked back at Dana.

"Would you try it? Rich's toy, I mean?"

"Not with some kind of memory lane program, no way. I worked my ass off to find a different path, you know? But with a movie, or a book? Sure. Maybe I could watch something that makes me believe it can actually be Christmas week when it's eighty-two degrees outside."

Michelle grinned and got out an actual smartphone rather than her little notebook.

"I doubt I can help you with the weather. I'm

more than twenty years out of St. Louis at this point, and it still seems weird to me. But I can get you into my department's holiday party tonight before you fly out of here tomorrow. You do *not* want to miss a bunch of cops cutting loose this time of year. Trust me."

Dana hesitated for a second, thinking of her half-hatched plan to curl up with her laptop, some variety of local cocktail, and a video call with Andre. Catching up on gossip and nerdy talk, especially about his own fabulous new job.

But they could catch up in person in less than twenty-four hours.

And the thought of a crazy police party was too good to pass up.

"As long as I can hang out in the corner and observe," she said, getting out her own phone for the address, "you're on."

KARI KILGORE

AUTHOR OF THE SOUND OF MURDER AND THE TECH EMPATH

MELTING POINT

A Dana Sanderson Short Mystery

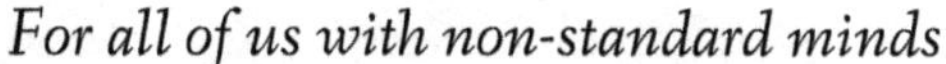
For all of us with non-standard minds

MELTING POINT

As temporary office spaces went, Dana Sanderson had to admit this one wasn't bad.

Modern chairs, adjustable in every possible direction, covered in soft blue leather. A sleek rectangular conference room table that had plenty of room for those five chairs, but didn't take up so much space no one could walk around it.

A gleaming steel pitcher waited in the middle of the table, surrounded by tall, sturdy glasses that made Dana smile. They were exactly like the highball glasses in her favorite restaurant nearby, all the way down to the little dimples around the middle for better grip.

More importantly, a side table held a carafe made of the same steel as the water pitcher, but filled with smooth, rich coffee. She'd already taken advantage of an orbital array of big blue mugs with every coffee condiment known to humanity tucked in around the edges.

Perfect for a former code wrangler and IT geek who'd happily gotten used to working from home with a fabulous career change. Then occasionally had to show up for meetings earlier than she was used to and wrangle her sleepy brain.

A wall of windows offered a second-floor view of a pleasant city park—with trees and flowers and even playground equipment—rather than an endless vista of mirrored building windows. Or worse, a cramped cubicle with no windows within fifty feet. One of the many advantages of being in tree-lined, residential Decatur rather than bustling downtown Atlanta or a soulless office park in the suburbs.

Rather than dull, generic art, the other walls held vivid photos taken within a few miles of the office. In Decatur, that meant sprawling live oak trees, idyllic bike paths, and funky-cool shops and restaurants. Including Dana's favorite pizza joint.

All the satellite offices for the Gossalor Insurance Group maintained a meeting room every bit as nice as this one, with most of the same supplies and atmosphere. All over Atlanta, out into the distant suburbs, and dotted here and there around the Southeast.

Each and every one of them available to Dana as Gossalor's special investigator in the fraud department, specializing in cybercrime. She remained grateful (and a little bit surprised) on a daily basis for the still-unbelievable turn of events that rescued her out of the oblivion of endless code crunching and life in a dreary cube farm.

Her younger self who worked so hard to put the bad old days of teenaged hacking in the past never would have imagined a day when those exact skills catapulted her into a job she loved. A job with a real future.

That younger self would have been even more stunned to realize uncovering an extortion ring based on subliminal mind control disguised as self-help meditation would be the key to her new life.

Even when this specific day in that new life started out with oversleeping: a rare and annoying feat for her despite her changeable schedule.

Dana currently wished for a mirror to make sure her ornery brunette hair hadn't corkscrewed itself into some sort of angular modern art display in the fierce August humidity. Her abrupt awakening meant she'd rushed out of the house without time to dry it.

She figured her usual nice jeans, charcoal-gray jacket, and nerdy t-shirt would look fine. Especially with her habit of only buying clothes that would go together in a pinch.

The roller coaster of jolting awake in a panic and careening out the door to get here by eight-thirty was bad enough. Getting stuck in hurry up and wait mode at going on...nine-fifteen was every bit as jarring as that instant panic when she opened her eyes.

Dana had her phone out to call the main office when a woman opened the meeting room door. Her black-streaked-with-silver hair was pulled back into a ponytail, a lovely contrast to her dark skin. She reminded Dana of friends of hers from Spain.

The woman wore a typical summer-weight law enforcement uniform of navy blue slacks and a lighter short-sleeved shirt. A lanyard badge around her neck identified her as working forensics for Cobb County, Georgia, to the northwest of where they sat.

Like many of the forensics folks Dana encountered during her investigations, the woman carried an overall relaxed and happy air, as if she did something light and fun like blowing bubbles for kittens and puppies for a living.

Dana had always wondered about that.

"You're the investigator?" the woman said. "From the fraud department? I'm Mira Cassoni."

"Yes ma'am, Dana Sanderson. The higher-ups usually send me out when a case comes along that doesn't fit their expectations."

Mira let out a big laugh at odds with her delicate features as she put a sturdy brown briefcase on the table beside Dana.

"If anyone had expectations for the bizarre things I've been seeing lately, it would be the woman we hauled into custody a few days ago on an unrelated charge. And she ain't talking."

She leaned forward with her hands on the table before going on.

"Listen, Dana, I know I was last-minute in getting in touch with you, then I left you hanging. I couldn't even share the case files so you could get started on your review last night. I was waiting on the approval, which made me late. I'm sorry about that. I won't take up any more of your time than I have to. But I do have to get a cup of coffee first."

It was Dana's turn to laugh and hold up her own half-empty mug.

"This is my second, and probably not my last for the day."

A quick minute later, Mira settled into the chair

beside Dana, fragrant cup of pale, cloudy coffee in hand.

"First things first. What brought you to my attention was partly the insurance policies our victim had. With Gossalor Insurance Group. You're top-flight on cybercrime for sure. But more than that, word gets around about the weird cases you've solved for Gossalor. That murder by meditation thing, and the drug hypnosis ring down in Miami. You see things in a different way aside from the cybercrime, and that's what I need here."

Dana wanted to protest. To say her best friend Andre had done most of the work on the first case, and good luck and a great detective had handled most of the second. But Andre himself would throw his signature epic side-eye her way if he heard her talking like that.

Not taking credit for her own hard work and skills.

Again.

It was hard for her to admit more often than not, but he had a point about that.

"Fair enough," she said, hoping she wasn't blushing. "This isn't the first time someone's told me my mind isn't quite standard issue. Tell me what your case is about, and I'll do my best."

Mira smiled, and Dana couldn't help smiling back.

"Okay, here's what I've got. This one's bugged me since we worked the scene this past week. Connie Belson. Her file would have landed on your desk soon, since she had a pretty big policy with Gossalor. Nothing strange about that part, at least not to my eyes. Got the policy about seven years ago when her niece was born, added another with the nephew a couple of years later. Right now, her brother is the beneficiary. He understands it's for the kids."

Dana nodded. "So she wasn't in the two-year contestability range, no problem there. But yeah, I would have been in on the investigation into the brother. Rotten business since beneficiaries are usually innocent, but part of the process. From the sound of it, you don't expect him to be involved, either. So what bugged you about it?"

"For one, the same thing that would have bugged your higher-ups once they got hold of this. A perfectly healthy young woman dropping dead for no good reason. The scene itself made my skin crawl. And, the way we connected this to a few other unusual deaths after hitting nothing but dead ends. The suspect I mentioned who isn't talking, that we picked up a couple of days ago? She had videos at her place."

Mira opened the briefcase, revealing the usual collection of notebooks and papers and about three hundred pens, but it was all neatly organized. What disturbed Dana was the big electronic tablet Mira pulled out and laid flat on the table.

"Hopefully not videos you're getting ready to show me."

Mira flashed a half-smile.

"Not into the weird stuff? Don't worry, this isn't our suspect's footage. This is from the forensics walkthrough on Connie Belson. The *suspect's* footage showed Ms. Belson walking into her own bedroom and hitting the floor. Seeing an unsolved murder play out was bad enough. What made it a hell of a lot worse was seeing almost the same scene play out in videos from five other houses. Two women and three men."

"Can you tell me what you picked up the suspect for?"

Mira activated the tablet, bringing up a full-color replica of the badge she wore.

"Sure. Our suspect had several bank accounts that weren't nearly as well-buried as she thought. Six to be exact. I wasn't on the forensics team for that one, but they brought me in when they saw Ms. Belson on the video. The strange thing is every person died the same way. Most at home, a couple in their cars. They pretty much took a breath and checked out."

Dana frowned. "That's awful, but I'm not sure I understand. I'm the one you'd call in to find those bank accounts most of the time, no matter how well they're buried. Or like I said earlier, to make sure the beneficiaries don't have something shady going on that we should know about. I'm not trained in murder investigations or forensics. And you think you've got your criminal already."

Mira took a long drink of her coffee, staring out over the trees outside before she focused on Dana again.

"We've got the suspect, sure. Sitting in lockup, smug as hell, and not saying a word. What we need from you, Dana, is how on earth she *did* it."

Dana drew back, blinking. "Me? I'm just an insurance investigator. This is your field, not mine. Surely the GBI has people on this."

"They do. And they're coming up empty so far. Some of these cases are months old. They're afraid as much as we are that this woman had a longer list of people she was paid to knock off. And you're right. Someone will probably find it sooner or later. Eventually."

Mira took a deep breath and closed her eyes for a few seconds.

"They'll probably find it," she said, "but until then, people will be walking around with no idea what's waiting for them at home, in their cars, maybe at work. Who knows? Even if we *find* the list, we still might not be able to protect them. Hell, they may not all be single like Ms. Belson, either. I'm wondering what would happen if someone else had walked into that bedroom instead. Like maybe if her niece or nephew had."

Dana stared at the image of Mira's badge on the tablet, pursing her lips. She had dug into impossible cases more than once, caught things no one else had seen. Found things bad people thought would never be found.

The one time in her life that her childhood skills as a hacker actually did somebody good.

Mira leaned closer and spoke in a low voice.

"Listen, Dana, I know I'm throwing a lot at you. But people here at Gossalor recommend you highly, and everyone I've talked to in law enforcement agrees. I need someone with a non-standard mind on this one. Someone who makes the strange connections, and the sooner the better. At least take a look, huh?"

Dana held her breath for several seconds, then let it out in a rush.

"All right. I'll do my best. Show me what spooked

you when you worked the scene at Ms. Belson's house."

Mira nodded and activated the tablet. She brought up a video, labeled with the address, date, and case number. Then the exterior of a typical suburban house, fairly new development. White siding, black fake shutters, two stories with an attached garage.

"The whole place was eerie," Mira said as the camera entered the house. "Looks like a model home for one thing. You know, the ones they decorate straight off the shelf for people to tour? They end up looking more like a hotel lobby than where someone would actually live."

The images on the screen were exactly that.

Beige walls in each room, except for one shocking "accent wall" in each. A bold primary color that only pointed out how dull everything else was. Matching tan couches and chairs, shelves and end tables that held bland trinkets, arrangements of candles in neutral colors, and not much else. Even the kitchen was oddly devoid of evidence that anyone lived there, with spotless gray granite countertops, an empty drying rack, and blue dishtowels hanging at perfect angles.

Dana wouldn't have been surprised if the row of

white cabinets with black handles only held empty boxes inside.

"Yeah, my realtor tried to get me interested in the glories of suburban living," she said. "My style is apparently more like a hundred-year-old bungalow that always needs...interesting repairs."

"Same here. No cookie-cutter suburbs for me. They kinda creep me out. Now, not much to see until we get to Ms. Belson's bedroom. The house had a kind of strange cinnamon and patchouli smell, but that was it. Cold as an icebox, too, more than most places even in an Atlanta summer."

Mira tapped the double arrows to fast-forward through a dining room and a guest room, then slowed back to normal speed.

Dana wasn't surprised to see a big bedroom as eerily perfect as the front of the house. This time the accent wall was a soothing midnight blue, and situated to catch the setting sun. All the décor, area rugs, and the bedclothes played off that one vibrant shade.

Matching white nightstands, a small chair and table, shelves at precisely varied heights around the walls. A similar variety of forgettable knick-knacks as in the living room, all looking like it was bought brand new yesterday.

Everything arranged as neatly as out front, too, as

if Ms. Belson (or a corporate decorator) had used a ruler to place every single thing.

That all made the thick indigo comforter pulled halfway onto the floor more striking.

"Didn't find a thing out of place on the body any more than in the house," Mira said. "Nothing except the blanket pulled off the bed. That happened when she fell according to our suspect's video. The rest of the bed would have passed inspection in any fancy hotel in the world."

Mira was right. The big pillows on the queen bed were still perfectly arranged, as was the robin's-egg-blue sheet. Only a couple of the accent pillows in varying shades of blue and purple were a bit out of place, as if someone had tried that old trick of pulling a tablecloth out from under a fully set table.

"She was on the floor right there," Mira said, as the camera zoomed onto an oval rug with swirls of the same two colors as the pillows. "This pretty little rug cushioned her fall, but I don't think she cared a whit by the time she hit the floor. That's almost all we got that day."

Mira hit pause on a closeup of the thick pile of the rug, with a faint impression that easily could have matched a body. Shoulder there, hip here. A clear mark of a foot and another of a hand.

Ms. Belson couldn't have moved much after she

fell, and the investigative team and coroner must have moved her very carefully when they took her away.

Dana shook her head.

"Well, I'm not sure what I'm supposed to see if none of you found anything. This was what, a couple of days ago? You say she was in good health. How did the autopsy look?"

"The initial results were clean. No drugs that they usually check for, no signs of trauma. They're still waiting on several tests, but those were all standard for what looked like so-called natural causes. Honestly, they ordered more tests once we linked this to the other cases with the suspect's videos. The chief medical examiner is holding everything until the new results come in. With one this strange, he insists on one combined report. Can't say I blame him. In this case, shit *can* roll uphill."

Dana snorted before she could stop herself. "That's exactly why they usually call me in with a policy this big. You're the one who wanted to bring me this, so I'm guessing you're a senior tech, not fresh out of school. You said something bugged you about this scene before the suspect and her videos turned up."

Mira tilted her head to one side and stared at Dana for a few seconds before she spoke.

"You saw the candles all over that place, right? The kind most people would say were too damn expensive to burn. All of them perfect, not a mark on them. But still, that smell."

"Cinnamon and patchouli."

"Right, all over the place, but not strong like incense. I'll add that Ms. Belson's big bathroom right around the corner from where she fell was as...shall we say compulsively neat as the rest of the house. But in there, there wasn't a trace of any kind of perfume or smelly bath salts or even scented deodorant."

She paused, and Dana took the cue to nod before Mira went on.

"What to guess what the bedroom and especially that comforter smelled like that day?"

Dana wrinkled her nose at the thought of it.

"Same cinnamon and patchouli as the rest of the house. But that comforter was a hell of a lot stronger?"

Mira nodded, and her smile was grim.

"The rug was the same, and one of my buddies who was first on scene said the body stank of it. One more thing I'll point out that *my* higher-ups wouldn't take seriously, then I'll leave you to your hunches. See the chest-of-drawers over there?"

She unpaused the video, and the camera zoomed in front of a tall unit beside the bed, oak with brass handles shaped like leaves from the same tree. A basket of oversized acorns made of pale woven grass beside a stack of leather-bound books with perfect, unbroken spines.

And another cluster of untouched fancy candles.

Except for one.

This one looked as thick as Dana's wrist and about six inches tall, made of charcoal gray wax with a rough texture. The camera raised up to reveal a deep circle in the very top. What she'd expect from a candle that had been burned.

But the depression was unusually smooth and shiny, with the wick too tall and pure white. Almost like someone had scooped out the wax there with a hot spoon, being careful to leave the surface neatly polished.

"Did that candle have the same stink as the rest of the house?" Dana said

She was surprised to see Mira blush.

"It did. Fainter though, not stronger like you'd think. That could have been because it was so damn cold in there. But then I remembered this kinky thing I heard about where people use candle wax during... well, during sex. And some of them melt into massage oil. No fingerprints on that candle, and the brand name carved into the bottom is the same as the others. That company doesn't make sex candles, so I don't know. I'm probably way off-base. But only the one candle touched in the whole big house and the body having that smell struck me as odd."

"I'd say that's worth filing away," Dana said. "If your team hasn't gotten it analyzed, I can do that. My best friend works in a private lab. He can usually slide things in for me."

"I suggested that right there on the scene, but I couldn't get anyone to sign off with what they thought was nothing more than a strange but natural death." Mira rolled her eyes.

"Apparently nothing like that was found at the other locations," she went on. "So they're still not listening. The fact that all of us worked that room with nothing more than simple face masks and walked away just fine didn't help. Myself, I wonder if our suspect was planning to go back and clean up the scene. And we picked her up before she got the chance. But all I got was a bunch of murder by candle jokes for my efforts."

She winked at Dana, then opened her briefcase again and reached into a boxed-off section in the top half. She pulled out a charcoal gray candle, zipped up inside an evidence bag.

"Checked it out on the way over here. That was part of what made me late."

Dana smiled. "Well, you were right in saying my

first case was murder by meditation, so I'm right with you on the candle. I'll see what I can find out. Did you find anything upstairs?"

Mira shuddered this time.

"There was *nothing* upstairs. I mean, there were three bedrooms and a couple of baths, but not a stick of furniture. Not even towels or toilet paper in the bathrooms. Bizarre if you ask me. Why have this big place and decorate the downstairs, then leave everything blank up there?"

"Did she live here long?"

"That's the thing, she was here for two years." Mira shook her head and held out her hands. "Makes no sense. It's like she moved in halfway and stopped. Or it was partly set up for her and she never bothered to finish or change anything."

"This *is* exactly the kind of case that drives my bosses crazy," Dana said, rubbing her forehead. "Everything we find makes it make less sense, not more. Do you mind letting me know when that final autopsy does come in? Just in case. And I'd like to get a copy of that forensics walkthrough if you can swing it."

Mira took Dana's offered card and held out one of her own.

"A link to the video is already in your inbox. You'll hear about the autopsy as soon as I do. I'm hoping to hear about those unusual connections you make, too. I've seen a lot of strange things out there in the suburbs, more than most people would believe. But that one gave me the creeps."

When Mira left, Dana refilled her coffee mug, got out her absurdly fast and powerful laptop, and checked her email. Sure enough, Mira's message was waiting for her.

Dana tilted the plastic-bagged candle back and forth while the huge video downloaded, resisting the temptation to crack the bag open for a sniff. If Mira was right, she had no desire to breathe in whatever that candle was putting out.

The truth was Andre loved breaking up the routine of his work with something new and exciting. That was exactly how Dana had gotten him involved in a few of her past cases, including that original meditation murder.

He'd been such a vital part of solving that mess that Dana's company had given him a huge bonus, along with the go-ahead to help in the future when he could. That and a couple of other cases had helped get him his fantastic new job, too.

The candle would just have to wait for the professional.

A quick viewing of the whole walkthrough video convinced her that anything the least bit strange would be the key on this case. If the downstairs looked like the TV design team had just scurried out after staging for the Big Reveal, the upstairs looked like the original builders had walked out after their last task was complete.

All the paint and flooring and tiles and lights and outlets were perfect, and perfectly clean. Like no one had ever set foot up there, much less lived there.

Whatever it was—assuming *it* turned out to be anything besides a strange undetected physical problem, videos or not—had to be downstairs.

And Dana did indeed have a strong hunch that something else would turn up if she only knew where to look.

The only interesting thing she found was a closeup on a control unit in one of the downstairs hall closets, the kind of thing designed to handle a huge home entertainment system, several gaming systems, security system, computer networking, the works. A big central hub hung on one wall with inputs for all those things and more, looking kind of like a flat-screen TV that was square instead of rectangular.

Rather than the typical mind-boggling snarl of cables and devices shoved in every which way as homeowners added new devices and never bothered to clean out the old, all she saw was wires coming in from the HVAC system and out to the thermostat in the kitchen.

That, a standard issue but expensive camera system, an ordinary internet router, and a big backup power supply were the only things in the compact space.

"What I wouldn't give for a setup this nice at home," she said under her breath.

Dana didn't love the idea of driving through the late afternoon heat, especially after Mira's descriptions of the icebox interior of Connie Belson's otherwise unremarkable house. But the next logical step was Andre and his expert analysis.

And the way her non-standard brain sparked brightest in combination with his.

She finished her coffee, packed up the candle and her laptop, and headed out into the inferno.

BY THE TIME Dana fought her way through the usual nightmare of traffic in Midtown Atlanta and made it to Andre's lab just outside of Roswell, she was hot, agitated, and starving. The sun was already on the downslope of a long, late summer day.

But this time of year, Atlanta held onto the heat, resisting the effects of darkness or any kind of errant breeze that wandered down from the northern mountains.

The air conditioning in her hybrid car fought the good fight, of course. It never quite managed to keep up in August.

On days like this, Dana missed the brisk nights of her childhood in the mountains of Pennsylvania almost as much as she appreciated the lack of bone-chilling cold here in the winter. She did wish it would snow more often, despite the commuter-panic traffic nightmare that inevitably caused.

Thankfully Andre kept his office at the lab somewhere in the vicinity of a walk-in refrigerator. His new employers didn't mind the increased utility bill a bit if they even noticed.

They were happily making a mint supplying chemical analysis that didn't necessarily get the same kind of attention (or regulation) as state or university labs did.

Andre was a contrast to his bland workspace in every possible way. Where the walls, floors, and waist-high work surfaces were either a dull beige or flat white, he was joyfully flamboyant and colorful. His outfits never failed to impress and surprise Dana even after nearly twenty years of friendship.

Tonight he sported iridescent burgundy pants with a warm copper-hued shirt, effortlessly coordinated in a way Dana never could quite manage in her own wardrobe. The same colors accented the swirls and patterns trimmed into his tightly curled black hair, and even glittered from the cover of the pea-sized cochlear implant tucked behind his left ear.

Up until a couple of years ago, he'd matched the cover to his brown skin and grown his hair longer on that side to cover it up. Dana still got tears in her eyes sometimes at how he'd stopped hiding and started accenting what he called his bionic ear.

As usual, Andre grinned when he saw her, crossing the room for a quick hug.

"Honey, are you a sight for bored eyes," he said, rolling his. "Nothing going on around here today except the standard corporate boredom. Tell me you brought me something *good* in out of that heat."

"Well, I know I brought you something strange. We'll see if it's good or not."

Dana frowned when she pulled the clear plastic bag out. The charcoal gray candle looked just fine, which made sense. Hot and muggy as her car had felt, it was nowhere near enough to melt a candle.

But patterns of streaks and drops decorated the bag now, some of them still soft and pliable.

"What on earth have you got there?" Andre said, standing shoulder to shoulder with Dana. "A massage candle?"

"Why am I not surprised you knew about those? I'd never heard about them until today." Dana gave him the rundown of everything Mira had told her, especially the hunches. "I think she might have a point, and it's as good a place to start as any."

Andre grabbed her hand when she started to open the bag.

"No ma'am, not right here in front of me. Did you not just say this was from a probable *murder* scene? I thought so. Then there's no way I'm going to let you open it up and take a big whiff."

He opened a drawer and pulled out two full face masks, both like transparent bubbles that would fit tight against the forehead and throat.

"Can't I just use a smaller one?" Dana said, staring at the intimidating thing. "I won't even breathe in. Mira said she worked the scene in the bedroom with only a regular mask."

"Forget it, missy. It may not be smell, did you think of that? What if it gets in through your eyes, those mucous membranes all around there? We're going to wear gloves to make sure it doesn't touch our skin, and I'll put it into the machine before I open it. But you'll be wearing the mask if you want to stay. Got it?"

Dana sighed and handed over the bag in exchange for the weird mask.

"If you have a hidden security camera around here I'm going to kill you."

Andre slipped his own mask on and grinned.

"Nope, not hidden at all. You might want to turn to make sure all of them get your best angle." He jerked his chin up at the ceiling, where several tiny camera buds perched and observed. "They're all over the damn building except the bathrooms. At least I don't *think* there are any in there. Come on, Dana, on with it."

Dana pulled the mask over her head, bracing for the claustrophobic choke she usually got with anything that surrounded her face. She didn't know if it was the clear surface or Andre's insistence, but she managed to keep breathing.

Andre walked slowly toward one of the huge machines along the wall, holding the bag up toward the bright overhead lights in his blue-gloved hands.

The machines reminded Dana of vast copiers she'd seen at the insurance agency, taller than her waist and several feet long. She'd watched people put in a stack of paper, tap on the screen perched on top, and after rumbles and clacks and a huge cloud of hot machine and hot paper stink, a stack of stapled or even ring-bound booklets came out the other side.

Andre knew the chemical analysis machinery as well as Dana knew the ins and outs of pretty much every computer she'd ever used. As far as she was concerned, these gigantic and shockingly expensive beasts were from another planet.

"Just how hot was your car on the way over here, Dana? Did you drive without the AC for some insane reason?"

"No, of course not. It stayed muggy cause it's a swamp out there, but I'm not *that* crazy."

He lifted a lid on one end of the machine, a pale blue dome that looked kind of like the hood of a VW Bug, and slid the bag inside.

"Well, Dana my dear, candle wax needs to be at least a hundred degrees Fahrenheit to start melting like this. And most of it isn't melted at all. Just those drops here and there. I don't know what you dragged in here, but we're about to find out."

He pulled the seal of the bag apart and pulled the whole thing down, exposing the candle and some of the drops, then closed the lid. Dana stepped up beside him when he started working with the touch-screen perched on top.

"You said this was a murder scene." Andre spoke in a distant, unusually flat way that let Dana know he was concentrating. "Anything strange about the body? Any autopsy or toxicology results?"

"No complete autopsy yet. Not a sign of trouble on the outside, nothing on any of the screens. She was perfectly healthy as far as anyone could tell, if a bit dull in her decorating habits."

Just like she'd expected, that last bit jarred him out of his work focus for a good giggle.

"I've always suspected people could die of being dull, *Dana*. You might want to take heed of that."

Dana was braced for another round of teasing about her terminally boring lack of any kind of style when Andre tapped the side of the screen instead.

A red box flashed in the middle with the words "Toxin: Gas" inside.

"Now *that* is anything but dull," Andre said. "None of the tests have even started yet. This is the standard procedure built into these things. Was this candle just sitting out in the house?"

"Right there in the bedroom. Mira and a bunch of cops and investigators were in there with nothing but standard face masks."

Andre shook his head, rubbing the back of his neck.

"This is high-grade stuff. Not the kind of thing that gives you a headache and lets you walk away. From these levels, if we'd opened that bag, we'd be joining your client up at the Cobb County Deep Freeze."

Dana rubbed her arms, trying to calm the goose-bumps raised there.

"Then why didn't it hit Mira? Or anyone else who was there? From the readouts on the thermostat and what she said, the house was almost as cold as this office."

"Was that candle missing its top when the forensics techs grabbed it at the house?" he said. "Didn't look like it melted enough in the bag to make that divot on the top."

Dana leaned forward to peer at the candle under the little curved hood.

"I thought it looked like someone scooped part of it out on the walkthrough video. The wick isn't burned, not a bit."

A mellow chime binged, and a dizzying burst of letters and numbers filled up the display screen.

"Let's just take a look and see." Andre tapped the screen several times. "This is a massive compound, never seen anything quite like it. I'm nowhere near one of the serious chemistry geeks that wander around this place. I just run the machines better than the whole big group of them could put together. But what I *can* do..."

He sat down at a typical computer with two big monitors, one already showing the mess of symbols from the analysis machine's display. He copied the data, then dragged it to what looked like a database field on the other screen.

"...is look at the same reference materials they do," Andre finished.

Dana had been as bad at chemistry and biology as she'd been great at math and programming back in school. Even with the reference, she'd be lost in a second. Advanced degree or not, Andre had clearly had no trouble with chemistry and didn't still.

She wondered if she'd ever stop being grateful for her friend.

"What we've got here, Dana my dear, is a proprietary chemical. It's nowhere out in the suburban wilds of Cobb County, or it shouldn't be. Used in manufacturing, and not the environmentally friendly kind."

"What does that mean for this case, though? They've got the woman in lockup, so they can probably trace how she got it. We still have no idea of how."

Andre clicked through a few more fields, then grunted. He spun around in his chair with a satisfied smile.

"There you go. This stuff melts at twenty-seven degrees. And that's when you get your toxic fumes."

"Please tell me you're talking that Celsius nonsense," Dana said, trying not to scowl. "No matter how low Ms. Belson kept the AC, that house wasn't below freezing anytime in the last six months."

"Celsius it is. You know, like the rest of the planet. Since you're determined to be a century or so behind the times, that's about eighty degrees Fahrenheit. Easy enough to hit in this sweltering city of ours."

"Easy to hit in my car, yeah. But not in this house, Andre. It was freezing cold in there, and she had a big fancy…"

Andre smiled and settled back into his chair, crossing his arms.

"*There's* the Dana I know and love. What dots did you just connect?"

"The police had the forensics walkthrough footage," Dana said, grabbing for her phone so she could take notes. "But the suspect had footage that had to come from inside the house. Different angles, no movement. There was a video surveillance system, high-end just like everything else. Creepy to have one in the bedroom if you ask me, but some people put them everywhere."

"Some kind of kinky custom job, you think?"

Dana shook her head, leaning against the desk beside him.

"There was nothing custom there. Not a damn thing. It looked like the forensics techs wandered into a real estate display unit by mistake, you know? Or one of those awful long-term-stay hotels. I doubt she changed a single thing from the second she moved in. The whole upstairs was empty, not even a sheet of toilet paper."

Dana smiled, meeting Andre's gaze.

"I doubt she changed a *single* thing, Andre. Including the admin passwords."

Andre jumped up and kissed Dana's cheek.

"And once again, you show me just how much of a damn *genius* you are!"

Dana laughed, grabbing Andre's hand.

"No sir, I most certainly am not. But you and me together, we're unstoppable."

Mira Cassoni met Dana back at the meeting room at the Gossalor office in Decatur the next morning. A tray of decadent pastries and plump bagels had joined the coffee and water, along with everything a hungry person could think of to top those bagels.

A sure sign that both Dana and Mira's higher-ups were confident in their imminent success.

Mira wore jeans and a t-shirt now, same as Dana, and her black and silver hair fell loose around her shoulders. They sat in the same places as the day before, each with a steaming hot mug of coffee at the ready.

The feast would have to wait until the job was done.

Dana's high horsepower laptop was tapped into the HVAC monitoring company's records for the house over in Cobb County, waiting on distant, massive servers to cycle back to the correct date and time.

The day Connie Belson walked into her bedroom for the last time.

"So the toxin is what made the body smell like that?" Mira said, sounding more surprised than doubtful. "What our suspect had on top of that damn candle?"

Dana nodded, her eyes still on her screen.

"That's the reaction, yeah, but it carries whatever she added to it. Once the compound melts, you can smell it, but by then it's too late. Then it all comes back out in the body after death. Unless you, me, and Andre are all way off on this, she's about to go from suspect to all-but-convicted."

The HVAC database finally prompted Dana for a password. She typed in exactly what the forensics walkthrough picked up on a little white sticker on the side of the control unit.

User name: admin.

Password: HVAC_HomeZone_X385.

"And this is the standard on these units." Mira leaned forward, staring at the colorful numbers, charts, and graphs. "Anyone could get it from the box."

"Or off the internet." Dana clicked through the control screen until she got to the system's recent performance. "Same with label on the internet router. And the security camera server. Every bit of it sitting there wide open."

Mira sat back with her arms crossed. "I'll be damned. I may work in forensics, but my granny taught me not to speak ill of the dead. I still can't figure why Ms. Belson never bothered to change a single one of these passwords."

"What *did* she change? You saw the place on more than a video. It looks like someone backed up a truck full of display rooms and dropped them off. And there it is."

She tapped a drop in system usage from early in the day they'd called up, marked in dotted blue lines. A spike in temperature at the same time was marked in dotted red.

"Topped out at eighty-one degrees," Dana said. "Or as my friend Andre would prefer, twenty-seven degrees Celsius."

Mira tapped the data from later that day as it

crawled across the screen. "Then it all leveled out overnight before anyone knew what happened to Ms. Belson. Back to icebox levels by the time we got there."

"Andre said this chemical shouldn't be out loose in suburbia, ever. If you can track down the missing supplies of it, you'll have another big clue to how your woman operates. And anyone she might have been working with where they produce it."

"We already have teams with the police, GBI, and FBI going back over where the other victims were when they died. I'd bet you'll be right. She probably added this stuff to candles, deodorant, air fresheners, even lip balm. Anything that's a gel that she could get up to the right temperature."

Dana downloaded the HVAC data to add to the rest of her report.

"The car or office or whatever did the work for her most of the time," she said. "But since she got pretty complex here with hacking the HVAC, she might have done the same somewhere else."

She sent the data to the printer in the corner, listening for it to whir into life.

The idea of Connie Belson's entirely standard-issue house somehow felt more sad and lonely than it had before.

"I still don't understand one thing," Dana said.

"Any more than why someone would want to have her killed. Why didn't she change *anything* in her house?"

Mira shuffled through the stack of papers already in front of her, shaking her head.

"People she worked with said she did the same thing in her office. Or *didn't* do, I should say. Looked like no one worked there at all. I guess when you do something like old-school corporate mergers and acquisitions like she did, you don't expect to be in any one place very long. Once the business is running as razor-thin efficiently as possible, no matter how high the cost to the people who work there, you're out."

"I remember that going on a lot in the Nineties and later the Great Recession," Dana said. "The ones who got hired to down-size and right-size and what-ever other pretty words they had for taking a company apart around the employees. Great way to make enemies, too. If Ms. Belson was on the job that long ago, that's where I'd start."

Mira got up to retrieve the last printout, and snagged the tray of goodies on the way back to the table.

"I expect we'll find more of that kind of thing once we get our bad gal's list of future targets, if there is one. I expect she'll be a bit more eager to talk once she sees what you figured out. It's amazing what the possibility of a plea bargain can accomplish. I can't thank you enough, Dana. For working this through, and for trusting my hunch. That made all the difference."

Dana dropped one copy of the HVAC data on the stack in front of Mira, another onto her own stack.

"Your hunch was the key to the whole thing. And the rest wasn't just me. You have my friend Andre's contact information in the report. We make a great team. All three of us do."

"We do. I already shared info for you and Andre both. You never know when I might be in touch again."

"Happy to help." Dana paused in reaching for an absolutely gorgeous raspberry Danish. "You still on for our celebratory dinner tonight?"

Mira grinned and executed a seated half-bow, then grabbed a flaky croissant for herself.

"Pizza and beer on Gossalor's expense account? And a chance to meet this secret weapon best friend of yours? Even after the carb-fest I'm about to indulge in, I wouldn't miss it."

They laughed together, and Dana hoped she would hear from Mira again.

Insurance fraud investigation paid well, and it kept her busy enough.

But she would jump at the chance to dig into something odd and fascinating in a whole different area from time to time.

She touched the edge of her Danish to Mira's croissant.

"Good work here, Mira."

"Right back at you, Dana. And back at Andre, too."

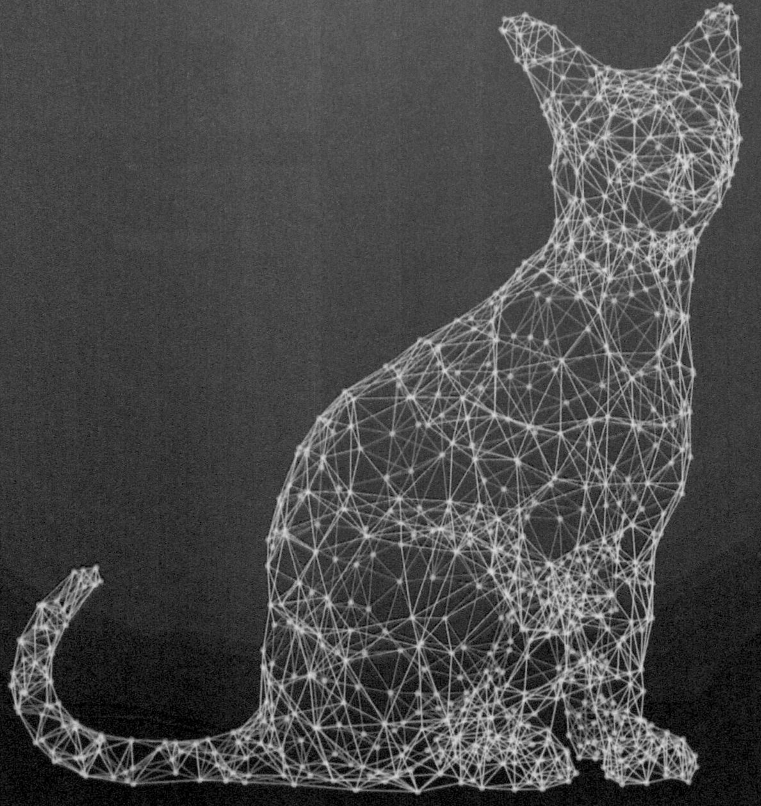

KARI KILGORE
AUTHOR OF THE SOUND OF MURDER AND THE TECH EMPATH

THREE COMPUTER
GEEKS GRUFF

A Dana Sanderson Short Mystery

*For everyone who's spent time
in the server room deep freeze*

CHAPTER 1

The last thing Dana Sanderson expected to hear when she walked into the IT dungeon at Gosalor Insurance was laughter.

Not the mad laughter of the insane, or the manic cackling of the condemned.

This sounded more like the honest, joyful outbursts of people out in the bright Atlanta sunshine, or maybe at a play or watching a kids' soccer game. About the furthest thing she could imagine happening in the dimly lit, freezing cold room full of little charcoal-gray cubicles set up in a rat-like basement maze.

Dana pocketed her tiny keychain keycard and brushed her shoulder-length brown hair back over her ear, dreading how it would get crackly and full of static in the dry air designed more for huge servers than human beings. Even in November, Atlanta stayed humid enough to mildew her uniform of black jacket and nerdy t-shirt while she was still wearing it.

Not a trace of moisture down here.

The usual aromatic combination of weapons-grade coffee and way too many pepperoni pizzas lingered despite the AC.

Another strange thing: Dana didn't hear the clashing of various music from the inmates of the cubicles, either. Only the low whir of a couple dozen servers and the rumble of constant airflow from the big air conditioners.

The current manager down here, Will McGranville, had a preference for light jazz that didn't match his age of Dana-didn't-actually-know-but-way-too-young-for-the-job. And her often-grumpy mentor Gayle, the only other person who was often down here, preferred classic rock played as loud as possible.

Upstairs where the actual business of insuring happened, all the blinding overheard lights stayed on. People chittered and chattered constantly, and too many of them wore enough perfume or cologne to drive a typical person crazy. Dana wasn't sure what it said about her that she'd preferred her time down here in the dungeon over her coding days up there in the noisy, bright, "normal" world.

And people sometimes wondered why she'd been so happy to escape Gosalor's hallowed halls and work from home.

The bizarre sound of laughter rang out again, and Dana surprised herself by smiling. She might be here on a break from her usual job of investigating insurance fraud, but she'd literally walked right into another mystery.

She pulled her sleek back laptop bag more comfortably onto her shoulder and ventured deeper into the warren.

Only a few desk lamps were on, along with not a single one of the overhead light bars. The raised floor echoed and shifted a tiny bit under Dana's feet even though it was covered in rubbery black matte tiles, just enough to make her feel uneasy. Like the troll under the bridge in "The Three Billy Goats Gruff" was about to jump out and gnaw on her ankles.

No overly eager head popped up over the wall of McGranville's cube, with his puppy dog eyes and bright grin happy to see anyone who'd ventured down into the IT den. So Dana turned left instead, heading toward Gayle's domain.

Dana slowed as she got closer to the warm glow of a desk lamp—the only light source other than ghostly green and blue monitor glow tolerated in this underworld. Now she heard the low murmur of not one voice talking to itself (a common symptom of people who worked more with computers than other people), but two.

And assuming the higher pitched one was McGranville and the lower was Gayle, the rise and fall of the voices was even more confusing. An actual conversation, as in one speaking, the other responding. Repeat. That instead of some variety of argument took her disorientation beyond strange, and directly to eerie.

At the clear and unmistakable sound of a meow, followed by more laughter, Dana froze.

Now she knew she'd crossed into some sort of bizarre alternate world.

Gayle and McGranville talking rather than fighting?

And a *cat* in the IT dungeon?

Her best friend Andre—far more fabulous than Dana could ever hope to be and possessing electronically superior hearing—would have likely been doubled over with his own raucous laughter by now. Dana only shook her head and kept walking.

The guts of Gosalor Insurance might not be her direct responsibility any more, but if someone was down here who shouldn't be, Dana wanted to know about it.

"Gayle?"

Dana couldn't hold back her own much quieter laughter as one head, then another popped up over the cubicle walls like demented prairie dogs. She recognized Gayle's short steel-gray hair and matching glasses, and Will McGranville's round face and disorderly brown hair.

But both of them were *smiling*.

"Dana!" Gayle said, waving her over. "You picked a great day to stop by."

Dana walked around the corner and gasped, unable to keep her mouth from dropping open.

Some species of gigantic gray striped naked rat sat upright right there on Gayle's normally spotless desk, staring at Dana with huge blue eyes and perked forward triangular ears.

When the rat let out a high-pitched *meow*, she finally realized she was looking at the cat she'd heard earlier.

Will grinned. "Meet our new mascot. Peluda."

"Did you say...Peluda?"

"Yeah," Gayle said, stroking the cat from its wrinkly gray forehead along its striped back. The cat's skin rippled under her touch. "My nephew has been rescuing cats and finding them homes for years. He heard about this little girl needing a home and decided it was high time I gave up my pet-free existence."

Dana slowly lowered her laptop bag to the floor, reached out her hand, and hesitated.

"Will she...Peluda, will she mind if I pet her?"

"Heck no, she loves it," Gayle said. "I think she stays cold even in this swampy climate to be honest. I might have to knit her a sweater before long, make sure she doesn't freeze all the time, especially in this meat locker."

Trying to force her understanding of Gayle the grumpy database expert into a world where she not only had a cat, but was willing and able to knit a *sweater* for said cat, Dana let Peluda sniff her fingers for a second. Up close, she realized the cat wasn't just gray, but had the distinctive tabby markings of an M on her forehead and sideways Fs on her cheeks.

Then she ran her fingertips down the same path Gayle had.

"She feels like a warm peach," Dana said, smiling. "I thought this kind of cat was hairless."

Gayle shrugged. "Mostly hairless. Enough that she hardly sheds at all. Suits me just fine."

Peluda stood under Dana's next stroke, raising her black and gray tail high. She chirped a few times, then jumped down and streaked off through the cubicle maze. Her tiny feet were silent on the rubbery tiles.

"I'm sorry," Dana said, turning to go after her. "I didn't meant to upset her."

Gayle waved her hand the way the cat had gone like an indulgent parent.

"No, she's good. She's been exploring all morning. It's not like she can get out of here or anything. Only one door, and only the three of us have access. Since no one ever comes down here anymore, I might bring her in a lot more often."

McGranville nodded, then glanced at his watch with a sigh.

"As far as I'm concerned, she can come in here every day. Livens up the place. Need me for anything, Dana?"

"Yeah, just a standard memory upgrade." She picked up the bag and held it out. "The latest OS can support more, so I figure it's time."

He took the bag, shaking his head.

"This thing is already superpowered. I'd love to have one like this myself at home."

He wandered off, happily telling himself about the specifications of the dream machine he'd love to build for himself.

Gayle looked at Dana, one bushy gray eyebrow raised.

"I'm guessing he has no idea what all that rig of yours can do."

"You're guessing right. Most of what makes it go isn't even in that bag. It's amazing what the new uplink technology can do."

They both turned at an inquisitive burble and low thud, going from low to high the same way a human asking a question did. Peluda stood on Gayle's desk again, tail held high and something black and shiny dangling from her mouth.

"What on earth have you found now?"

Gayle rubbed the cat's head and gently pulled the thing from her mouth. She adjusted her architect-style desk lamp, the kind with the arm hinged in the middle that always reminded Dana of some kind of luminescent creature.

Whatever Peluda had was stubby, about the size and shape of a thumb with one rounded end and one rectangular. A narrow LED screen showed a series of three numbers, a space, and three more. As Dana and Gayle watched, a minuscule progress bar ran down to nothing. A new series of numbers appeared, along with a full progress bar.

"Missing a VPN token?" Dana said, reaching into her pocket to make sure hers was there, still attached to her keychain along with the little keycard. She used hers for two-factor authentication and security when she needed to get to Gosalor's network assets.

She used her own more specialized security for her investigative work most of the time.

"No, not that I know of." Gayle set the little token on her desk, handing Dana a long, narrow wand with multicolored feathers dangling at the end. "Play with her, would you? Otherwise she'll bat this off onto the floor and take off with it again."

Sure enough, Peluda was already reaching out toward the token with one long-toed paw.

Dana wiggled the wand near the floor, and Peluda's pupils got so big the ring of bright blue almost disappeared. She jumped onto the floor and commenced aerial acrobatics trying to catch the feathers.

"This really is McGranville's department," Gayle muttered to herself as she peered at the back of the token, then typed away on her keyboard. "He's supposed to be getting these things organized after the disaster Billy Jones left behind on the way to getting himself sent to prison for larceny. How much time did that asshole end up getting, anyway?"

Dana tried to concentrate on twitching the feathers in just the right way to keep Peluda leaping and bouncing. That was far better than letting herself remember the day she'd accompanied the Georgia Bureau of Investigation to arrest her former co-worker for stealing from Gosalor.

Billy had laughed that day, but it had been far more manic than happy.

The strange undercurrent of relief in his voice and his face disturbed her most of all.

"He's in for fifteen years, probably less if he can manage to behave himself," she finally said. "At close to sixty thousand dollars and systems in place to get a whole lot more, he was easily into felony land."

"Yeah, well, can't say he didn't deserve it. Left an undocumented mess down here and an untrained kid who still hasn't managed to clean it up. Here, got it. The serial number on that token matches logins by Michael Rawson. Works up in the business assets department, covering big facilities, vehicle fleets, buildings."

"Any reason he should be down here?" Dana said. "When did he last log in?"

A few more taps, and many more graceful pirouettes and twists and leaps by Peluda.

"No, no reason at all that I can tell. Has a laptop, but he's had the same one for a couple of years now. Not everyone gets theirs updated every chance they get like you do. Last logged into the VPN network... looks like a week ago."

Dana tucked the feathered wand into her back pocket and picked up the purring cat. She felt like a rumbly velvet-covered furnace.

"How did his token get all the way down here? You'd think he would have missed it by now."

Peluda twisted in Dana's arms, then leaped onto Gayle's desk. She crouched low, staring back and forth between them with her eyes wide, then jumped down and dashed out of sight. This time Gayle and Dana laughed together.

"I swear that cat's half crazy," Gayle said. "That's why she likes it down here so much. Let me pull up his contact info and we'll call him."

Dana watched as Gayle navigated through screens, drilling down into databases that even she'd have trouble getting into from the outside.

And Dana could hack her way into almost anything.

Gayle sat back, rubbing her chin and staring at a bright red line on the screen.

"Huh. Looks like Mr. Rawson is under suspension. Hasn't reported to work at all for a week, or even called in. Still doesn't explain how this thing got down here."

She held the token up, turning the smooth black plastic back and forth under the lamp.

When Peluda jumped up on the desk this time, she held a heavy gold ring in her teeth. A man's college class ring, from the looks of it, with a big sapphire stone and lots of engraving.

"What the *hell*?" Gayle absently patted Peluda's head as she extracted the ring and held it up to the light.

A gold G with a T joined to it shone from the stone.

"Please tell me McGranville went to Georgia Tech," Dana said, trying to catch her breath through the falling sensation in her gut. "Please tell me that's his ring."

Gayle swallowed twice before she answered, her voice rough. "University of Georgia, I'm afraid. Definitely not twenty-six years ago like whoever wore this. I'm afraid to look at the inside of this ring, too."

But she did look, turning it over as Peluda purred and rubbed her velvety big-eared head against Dana's hand.

The engraving inside confirmed the ring was owned by one Michael Keith Rawson.

Currently missing and on suspension from Gosalor Insurance Group.

CHAPTER 2

After a fruitless search through the cubicles and the rows of servers at the back, Dana, Gayle, and even McGranville engaged in a rousing game of doing everything they could to get Peluda excited enough to fetch something else shiny. What finally worked was tossing the feather wand back and forth between them, then ignoring the cat entirely.

When she finally galloped back through the cubicles, they broke into the rather awkward and undignified run of many IT professionals.

Beyond the identical and mostly empty cubes, three rows of server racks took up the back of the room. Gleaming black boxes stacked one on top of the other—sort of like a bunch of expensive, blinking stereo equipment—sat in racks that stretched from just above the floor to the lowered white tile ceiling.

Dana, in the lead with her habit of long walks through the neighborhood with Andre in the evenings, turned down the last server row just as Peluda's slender, striped tail disappeared under one of them.

"There! She went under that middle one. There's space for cables and such beneath each server rack, right?"

McGranville stopped beside her, his round face flushed, Gayle close on his heels.

"Yeah, about a foot long, a few inches wide. Easily big enough for her to squeeze through. Make sure she doesn't climb out one of the other ones, and I'll go get the floor tile lifter."

"The *what?*" Dana said, raising her voice to talk over the much louder fan noise so close to the servers and huge cooling ducts under the floor. She knelt and put her ear almost against the rubbery tile, smart-phone flashlight in hand, peering into a gap of not quite a foot between the server and the floor. The matte tile had an opening just like McGranville had described. "All I see is a couple of cable bundles under here, but she could fit for sure."

"You can't just pick these things up," Gayle said, scuffing her heel against the tile by Dana's head. Each of them was a couple of feet across. "They're heavy and fitted together. Takes a special kind of tool, looks like suction cups on a stick."

What McGranville brought back did indeed look just like that. Two black suction cups, each wider than Dana's hand, attached to a metal bar. The whole thing hung off the end of a longer bar about the length of a broomstick with a sharply curved handle at the top.

"Are we sure we want to just yank that tile up?" Gayle said as Dana got to her feet and stepped back. "If it *is* Rawson? Or what's left of him?"

McGranville stopped with both suction cups pressed against the tile, his eyes wide.

"You don't think there's a *body* down there, do you?"

No one spoke for several seconds while the server lights blinked. Dana couldn't hear any sign of the cat, but the constant fan noise made it hard to hear herself think. The sinking feeling in her gut was stronger now, twisted through with worry.

"I don't know," Gayle finally said with her normal weary sigh. "Just get my cat out of there and we'll figure it out."

McGranville smacked the suction cups against the floor and lifted the tile straight up and to the side.

Peluda leapt out right behind it, this time holding

a key ring with three keys and a tiny metallic thumb drive in her mouth.

Dana didn't need her phone's light to see the body dumped on the concrete subfloor—on its side, neck swollen and bruised, against a wide air handler duct, one arm sprawled up across its chest, blue suit sleeve raked up to show a dead still wrist. When she did shine her light in, the wide pale line on his finger where the ring had been stood out.

The sinking feeling in her gut turned into clenching nausea.

"Holy shit," she whispered. "How did he get under there?"

McGranville backed up, shaking his head.

"No way. There's no way. This room is locked, you know. Secured. Does anyone else even *have* a keycard besides the three of us?"

Gayle scooped Peluda up. "The keycards get logged every time someone goes in and out. Supposed to, anyway." She pointed at white glassy bulges in the ceiling in the middle of each row. "Security cameras, too. This doesn't make sense."

"He doesn't..." Dana started, then took a deep breath. "He doesn't stink yet, and he eventually would even with all these air handlers. Can't have been under there long. A day at most."

"I don't care if it's a day or a week or fifteen

minutes," McGranville said, taking another step back. "He can*not* be under there!"

Gayle glanced up at the cameras again. She stepped close to Dana and held out her closed hand between their bodies. Without thinking, Dana held out her open one.

The keys and the jump drive dropped into her palm with a faint jingle, the metal chilled from its time under the floor next to a *corpse*.

Dana swallowed a couple of times before she could speak.

"Why do you think I would want his *keys*?"

Gayle shook her head, looking at the gap in the floor instead of at Dana.

"Not the keys," she said in a low voice. "Got a strong hunch you might find something." She raised her voice. "Come on, McGranville. Let's all get away from here. Dana needs her machine, and I need to get Peluda out of here before a bunch of cops come stomping in."

He jerked his head toward her. "Cops? You think we should call the cops?"

"We have to," Dana said. "Building security, too. I'm not about to get into the body hiding business. Looks like somebody's better at it than I could ever be anyway. Listen to me, Will. How would that work? Will? What would you guess?"

She was curious, sure, but she wanted her computer back and all in one piece, upgrade or not.

She had exactly zero desire to be cooped up inside a crime scene. She'd seen more than enough from photos and video and evidence bags to know she'd be fine missing the live-and-in-person version.

He stared at Dana for a second, then blinked and shook his head.

"They would... I guess if someone could get in here without us knowing, which they can't, they'd have to go around to the back, by the wall. There's room enough to walk around, and it would make sense by the angle of...of the body. The rest of him must be under the server, yeah."

He nodded, then seemed to realize what he'd just been saying. He squeezed his eyes closed for a second and turned away.

"I'll get your machine ready, Dana. I know you'll want to get out of here. But maybe you could call it in first? Please? I'd really appreciate that."

Dana turned to Gayle after he walked away.

"You may want to just stash Peluda in her carrier for now, Gayle. There are cameras here, and the cardkey records, like you said. There's no reason you'd look suspicious."

Gayle stared down at the body under the floor, then back at Dana.

"You've got a point. You might want to slip that jump drive off the key ring, then. If they ask what all Peluda found, and they will, you and me can keep it straight. I'm not so sure McGranville can."

"I'm sure he can't," Dana said. "Let's dump the data off to one of your machines now, then transfer it to my rig before I leave. That way the cops can have at it and maybe I won't have to."

"*Sure* you won't," Gayle said, walking back toward the cubicles, nearly hairless cat in her arms. "Something like this happens at Gosalor's headquarters, right here in the heart of the whole operation, and they're not going to want their hotshot investigator to dig around? What do you think, Peluda? Yeah, me too."

Dana walked around to the back of the server rack, to the unpainted concrete wall a few feet behind the last row. The noise was even worse, and the same flat black tiles ran right up to the concrete. The light on her phone didn't show any kind of scuff marks or anything like that, but building security and the police would have much better tools than she did.

At least when it came to physical evidence.

Dana liked her own expertise just fine when it came to zeros and ones.

CHAPTER 3

The worst part of the initial security and police investigation was the overhead lights.

For the first time in all the years Dana had been venturing down to the IT dungeon, all of the painfully bright light bars and bulbs and domes and everything else were on.

It made sense, of course, with several uniformed Gosalor security guards and what seemed like a whole police squadron poking around at the back of the room, then wheeling the mystery body out on a stretcher.

But the glare induced instant headache for her, Gayle, and McGranville.

Thankfully he'd recovered his senses enough to get her upgraded machine back, and Gayle transferred the jump drive's data and added the key ring to the little pile of evidence before anyone else showed up.

The officers' questions were calm and polite, unlike some of the recorded interrogations Dana had seen. But their questions got repetitive, fast.

The only one who didn't have a strained expression by the time it was all over was Peluda. She curled up inside her curved blue plastic carrier with a blanket draped on top, freshly cleaned miniature litter box tucked into the back corner, purring every time the guards and officers stopped by to tell her what a good kitty she was.

After they cleared Dana and the others to go, one of the police officers she'd worked with on other cases pulled her aside.

Mira Cassoni was a few years older than Dana, with her black-streaked-with-silver hair pulled back into its usual bouncy ponytail. For the first time since Dana had started working with the forensics investigator, Mira wore the jacket of her blue pantsuit rather than only a short-sleeved top.

"Any ideas from your side?" Mira said. "Your rather shaky IT manager said there's no way anyone got in and out of here without someone knowing. And exactly as your hard-as-nails database pro said, nothing shows up on the keycard reports. Video's clean, too."

Dana shook her head, rubbing the back of her neck.

"Damned if I know, Mira. I do know Gayle's rock solid, same as her reports. McGranville is young and freaked out, but he's telling the truth as far as I can tell. I never heard of this guy Rawson before today. I just picked a rotten day to stop by."

She focused on Mira.

"Anything from your side?"

"No doubt you'll get briefed as soon as your managers tell us to loop you in, so here goes. Besides a dead body, who *is* your missing Mr. Rawson, we're up against that concrete wall back there. He's been under the floor for less than forty-eight hours, but long enough to be chilled through to the brutal room temperature you have here. Marks and swelling around his neck look like strangulation."

Prickly chills raced over Dana's flesh.

"Did it happen here?"

"Hard to tell, but he at least died in a different position and stayed there for a little while. Blood's pooled on his back and his opposite side. Your HR department says he was suspended for not showing up or calling in for a week, nothing but good behavior for four years before that. He definitely wasn't killed as long as a week ago. And that's about all we've got. Only weird thing is the dust on the subfloor back behind that server wasn't disturbed enough for him to be shoved under there. It's like he dropped out of nowhere. We'll have someone crack into that jump drive on his key ring. I predict they'll then turn it over to you to crack in some more."

Dana felt a guilty flush about already having the data, but not bad enough to confess. Mira and Gayle were absolutely right.

Odds were high she'd be called in if anything the least bit strange showed up.

Especially in the heart of Gosalor operations.

"So you at least know how he was killed," Dana said. "But nothing on where or who or why, or how the hell he ended up here."

"That's pretty much it. Standard for most homicide investigations this early on, but this one is looking several degrees stranger than most. I'll ping you if I get more."

"I'll do the same. Thanks, Mira. Good luck on this one."

Gayle stopped beside Dana as the investigator walked out. She held Peluda's case, but the cat was no longer enjoying herself. The barely there fuzz on her forehead was deeply wrinkled, and she let out a long, plaintive *yowl* when she saw Dana.

"Me too, Peluda," Dana said. "I'm just glad they

got the poor guy out of here. How's McGranville holding up?"

"Eh, he's freaked out. More than I think is necessary, but he's just a silly kid. Sounds to me like nothing turned up so far."

"That's what I'm hearing, too. I'll take a look when I get home. Anything at Gosalor off limits as far as you're concerned, Gayle?"

"Not a thing. I made damn sure I kept anything I didn't want found off these networks once I realized how good you are, kid. A long time ago. Have at it."

CHAPTER 4

An hour later, Dana huddled up in her warm home office with hot chocolate, sweatpants, extra-thick socks, and an embarrassingly fluffy black housecoat. That blasted server room had chilled her through to the bone, every bit as much as finding a freaking corpse under the floor had.

She tried her best not to think about how her long-standing, Billy Goats Gruff-inspired discomfort with raised floors had now been entirely justified.

She'd escaped her bland apartment once Gosalor paid out for the first case she'd solved—saving them a fortune in the process—into a wonderful little bungalow east of the city. But this tiny little afterthought office had resisted her efforts at decoration. The walls were still bland beige, and no carpet covered the hardwood floor.

She had she same small, basic computer desk she'd had for years, and one of the black flexible-arm lamps like Gayle's. A couple of huge flat-screen monitors and a few external hard drives rounded out her standard equipment.

The only additions were her special work tools, carefully (and quietly) acquired on her own dime rather than Gosalor's.

What looked like a shiny black hockey puck blinked away on the desk. A lightning-fast and incredibly secure internet uplink. Beside that, an elongated slab of tan plastic showed only one glowing orange light. That device blocked any incoming interference or snooping through cellular, WiFi, and a bunch of other technologies and networks.

She didn't pretend for one second that her equipment couldn't be hacked or traced. She was too good at her day job and her youthful-hobby-turned-career of hacking to believe that. But she'd done enough to make sure anyone who managed wouldn't be a casual thief.

Dana also made sure she could wipe her super-laptop, smartphone, or pretty much anything else that came her way in seconds if needed.

She fired up her rig and dug into the data from the late Michael Keith Rawson's silvery little jump drive. A strong but easy enough (for her) to hack password fell in a matter of minutes.

Then two folders. Also locked, also fairly easy to pry into.

A bunch of locked Word documents, a couple of similarly protected Excel spreadsheets, and nothing else. Mr. Rawson probably thought he'd done a good job of securing his data, and for most situations, he had. The question was whether the files were related to his death, and if they'd been worth dying for.

She picked one of the Word docs at random and opened it.

The text was minuscule, even on the huge screen, and it spilled across from one side to the other with hardly any spaces or returns that she could see. She selected the whole document and changed the text from the absurd Garamond two point to good old Times New Roman twelve.

"What the hell did he get *into?*" she muttered, sitting forward.

The page was covered with line after line, row after row of what looked like some kind of corporate or industry report. Along with the initial insane font size, all the space after the ends of sentences had been removed. It was an eye-straining mess to read.

After a few passes with Find and Replace to

make the whole thing more legible, Dana sipped her cooling hot chocolate and scanned.

She'd only eaten a light dinner after the gut-churning events of the day, but before long she regretted getting even that much down.

What Michael Rawson had been into was an especially nasty collaboration between a few small, independent insurance agencies and a handful of coroner's offices in various counties. Some in isolated rural areas, some in overburdened areas of cities like Atlanta, Columbus, and Augusta. A few doctors were named in the reports, too.

They'd all been working together for the last eight years to defraud the victim's families on life insurance claims, and quite successfully from the looks of the Excel files. The coroners would write up whatever it took to invalidate the payouts, and the doctors backed them up.

Starting within the last two years and increasing rapidly, the ring had advanced to actually *causing* the victims' deaths right before payout milestones in the policies. With coroners and doctors covering up the murders.

And the newest twist, within the last few months, had ghost policies written when the victim signed up. The agencies backed each other up, the doctors handled the medical exams, and in a few cases, the payouts had been collected and banked.

In other words, a complex and sophisticated ring of fraud that hit at the very heart of the entire industry, not to mention the safeguards of doctors and coroners.

From the dates on his files, Rawson had started compiling his information over the last several weeks. After a bereaved family member asked him about their policy payouts being denied.

Now that family was about to be bereaved all over again, if they weren't already.

His last note, dated less than a week ago, detailed his suspicions that someone within the ring had caught on to what he was doing. Michael Rawson had dropped out of sight only hours before he'd planned to turn the whole thing over to the police, state authorities, and the FBI.

Dana sat back, shaking, not sure whether she should reach out to Mira Cassoni or not.

She knew from past experience that Mira and her colleagues at her department and at the GBI were sharp and competent. They'd worked together enough to prove that.

And the truth was she didn't want to have to bring this to them or testify. Partly to avoid the whole horrifying business, sure. But she'd had enough experience during her run-ins with law enforcement as a young hacker to know she didn't want to get involved with these kinds of criminals.

Deeply frightening time spent with violent offenders her own age back then had scared her straight more than anything else.

At that moment, Dana wished more than anything else that Andre wasn't out of town, or maybe that she had a warm critter to cuddle with. As delightful as Peluda was, a cat of any variety would do.

She jumped and let out a little screech when her smart phone vibrated on her desk.

Mira.

Break on why - nasty vicious stuff. Proceeding on that front. Hoping you can help us out with how in the morning.

Dana picked up her phone, surprised that her hands only trembled a little. The gigantic surge of relief had her very breath shaking in her body.

Glad for progress, see you then.

She shut everything down then, with no desire to go digging into the databases and records she could access from home.

Not tonight.

Tonight she'd be heading straight for mindless TV, valerian tea, and hopefully an early, dreamless sleep.

With no nightmares about being trapped under the server room floor.

CHAPTER 5

Mira's grim, determined face told Dana everything she needed to know as soon as she walked into the IT dungeon the next morning. Neither Gayle nor McGranville were there.

Dana doubted Mira had told either of them about the contents of Michael Rawson's jump drive.

Hell, Dana might have to pretend *she* didn't know about that.

Dana thought she might just break down and cry at the sight of a huge carafe of coffee from the wonderful shop just down the road sitting in one of the cubes. That heavenly smell alone was enough to perk her up after what turned out to be a restless night after all.

"Dana," Mira said, already cradling her own

coffee tankard. "Thanks for joining us. I know it was a rough night for everyone. We've already mapped out the security camera's dead spots all along the outside walls back in the server room."

"Okay, good," Dana said, filling up her stainless-steel mug and taking a too-hot sip. "Hopefully we can get new cameras down here if nothing else. What can I do?"

"The keycard records for down here are still solid. Despite what your colleague Gayle calls your former manager's incompetence. And I had another look at the subfloor back there. I was right about the dust being hardly disturbed. No one *dragged* him under there."

Dana took another sip, shaking her head.

"Then I don't understand why I'm here."

Mira stepped closer.

"Michael Rawson was after some bad people, Dana. Really bad people who got away with it for a while. That part's being handled thanks to him. But I have the feeling at least one more person was in on this who we're not seeing. I want you to see if you can get into the HVAC records for our targets."

"HVAC... Why me?"

Mira shrugged. "I don't have evidence for that, not yet. Can't justify it, especially not when they're under intense investigation for some terrible things. I'm afraid they'll ditch those records when they realize what's coming."

Dana couldn't think of any reason to refuse, and what she'd read the night before gave her all kinds of reasons to do this.

If she could help get every single person involved brought down, she would.

"Give me the list."

The systems for the Mira's targets—the same Dana already knew—were protected far less than Michael Rawson's data had been. For this part of their records, anyway. She suspected the information about their crimes was far better hidden, but not beyond the reach of the agencies already breathing down their necks.

In less than half an hour, Dana had the name of the HVAC contractor, and access to *those* records.

Including maintenance visits to Gosalor Insurance Group's headquarters over the last week.

"Those big ducts," Dana said. "Under the floor. That's how they dumped him, isn't it?"

Mira took a deep breath and let it out in a long, coffee-scented sigh.

"Has to be. No telling who else or what else has been dealt with the same way. Hell, this group might have been planning something else here. And now you've given me enough to know which records to get *from* here to prove it, and to snag the asshole who did it. That's one less evil fuck to worry about starting the whole thing up again someday."

Dana nodded, the stress of a long day followed by a difficult night draining from her shoulders and neck.

"I'm just glad this is over."

"You did a good thing just now, Dana. I appreciate it more than you know. I hope I get a chance to make it up to you someday."

Dana smiled. Something about the long, long hours of the night before had shifted her feelings about living alone, even after years of doing just that.

Not nearly enough to put up with a person, no.

But a certain purring, peach-fuzz kitty had crossed her mind more than once.

"Maybe you can make it up right now," she said. "You live pretty close to me, right? I'm thinking about getting a rescue cat or two from Gayle's nephew. Maybe you can help me find a good vet close by. And a local pet supply shop so I can spoil them silly."

Mira let out a laugh that no longer sounded quite so odd in the IT dungeon.

"You'll love my vet," Mira said. "She's great with

my crazy cats and big goofy dog. But you *know* you won't get a chance to spoil those kitties yourself once Andre's back in town."

"Maybe not," Dana said, smiling. "But I'm going to do my level best to keep up."

www.KariKilgore.com

ALSO BY KARI KILGORE

I hope you enjoyed reading the stories in *Hacking Cybercrime* as much as I enjoyed writing them. More adventures with Dana and Andre are on the way!

To jump into another tale of women in tech at the height of their powers, check out *Team Building Revenge*.

For more mystery and crime short stories, along with novellas and novels, visit www.KariKilgore.com/Mystery. If you enjoy stories from near-future all the way into science fiction, check out www.KariKilgore.com/ScienceFiction.

Check out more of my fiction, including almost every genre, and be first to hear about release dates, Kickstarters and other fun projects, and exclusive e-book and print editions at www.KariKilgore.com.

Dispatches from the Galaxy:

Restricted Species

The Becalmed

Plurapod Pathogen

The Changes Cascade

Near Future Forward (with Jason A. Adams)

Dispatches from the Galaxy: A Space Opera Novella Trio

Dangerous Days on a Pleasure Planet

Novels:

Until Death

The Dream Thief

Hand Me Downs

Protecting Her Own

The Coffee Bomb and the Corporate Spy

The Great Gold Record Heist

Novellas:

Legacy of the Land

In the Pines

Fantastic Women: A Dark Fantasy Novella Trio

DNA Never Lies

The Box of Possibilities

Murder at the Fabulous Feline Emporium

Team Building Revenge

Storms of Future Past:

Dreaming the Storm

Joining the Storm

Into the Storm

Fighting the Storm

Storms of the Heart

Storms of Future Past Omnibus

Voices Through Time:

Songs in the Mountain

Secrets in the Land

Sorrows in the Earth

Walking the Ghosts

The Odd Society:

Independent by Means of Magic

Protected by Means of Magic

Collections:

Fantastic Shorts: Volume 1

Fantastic Shorts: Volume 2

Fantastic Shorts: Volume 3

Escape into Romance

Stepping Out of Reality

Facing Down Extraordinary

Investigations Beyond Belief

Passages in the Real World

Fantastic Side Trips

A Kaleidoscope of Cat Tales

A Tapestry of Holiday Tales

Aunties Among Us

Four-Legged Heroes

Anthologies *with Jason A. Adams*:

Partners in Romance

Shadows Mountain Deep

Uncommon Holidays

Partnership in Crime

ABOUT KARI

Kari Kilgore's wanderlust and imagination lead her all over the world on grand adventures. Her heart and family bring her home to her native Appalachian Mountains of Virginia. From that solid base and with the help of the ever-changing lens of her imagination, she brings those adventures to life in fiction.

While the people, places, and events in these stories are fictional, she's eternally grateful to her own real-life versions of Andre and Gail for helping her survive the IT grind.

Kari writes mystery, contemporary fiction, science fiction, romance, and fantasy, and she's happiest when she surprises herself. She lives with her husband and fellow author Jason A. Adams (another cubicle escapee), various house critters, and wildlife they're better off not knowing more about.

The Confidential Adventure Club

For Kari's exclusive free After The End stories and deleted scenes, discounts, early releases, adorable pet photos, Kickstarters and other fun projects, Spiral Publishing Exclusive Edition e-books and print books, and a whole lot more not available anywhere else, join us in The Club.

Hope to see you there!

www.KariKilgore.com
www.SpiralPublishing.net
www.ConfidentialAdventureClub.com

BB bookbub.com/authors/kari-kilgore

a amazon.com/author/karikilgore

g goodreads.com/karikilgore

f facebook.com/kari.kilgore.1

ADDITIONAL COPYRIGHT INFORMATION

The Sound of Murder

Copyright © 2018 by Kari A. Kilgore

All rights reserved

Published 2018 by Spiral Publishing, Ltd.

Book and cover design copyright © 2018 by Spiral Publishing, Ltd.

Cover art copyright © 2018 by Stepanenko Oksana | Dreamstime.com

ISBN-13: 978-1096207115

The Fabulous Feats of Billy

Copyright © 2021 by Kari A. Kilgore

All rights reserved

Published 2021 by Spiral Publishing, Ltd.

Book and cover design copyright © 2021 by Spiral Publishing, Ltd.

Cover art copyright © 2021 by milagli | depositphotos.com

Originally appeared in *Mystery, Crime, and Mayhem: Thieves,* Knotted Road Press, 2020

ISBN-13: 979-8-7116-5087-4

Glory Lane and the Humid Holiday

Copyright © 2021 by Kari A. Kilgore

All rights reserved

Published 2021 by Spiral Publishing, Ltd.

Book and cover design copyright © 2021 by Spiral Publishing, Ltd.

Cover art copyright © 2021 by arsija | depositphotos.com

When Self-improvement Turns Deadly

Insurance agency programmer Dana Sanderson only wants peace and quiet at work.
Then the investigation of a rash of suspicious natural death claims lands on Dana's laptop.

The Successful Launch of a Disaster

Billy's new tech start-up sits on the verge of greatness. A fantastic reward for leaving his rotten old job in the dust.
Until a miscalculation lands Billy in a nightmare.
Unfortunately Billy's way out puts him squarely in cybercrime expert Dana Sanderson's sights.

A Strange Case in a Strange Place

A chance to recapture past glory days gone awry.
A cybercrime expert forced to endure warm, sunny weather in December.
A South Florida holiday with two stressed-out techies in the wrong place at the right time.

An Invisible Countdown to Death

A cookie-cutter suburban house. A strange aroma. A dead body. A suspect refusing to talk.
Sometimes a stumped investigation needs a non-standard mind.

When the Cat Drags in a Mystery

A cold IT dungeon, full of noisy servers and grumpy workers. Not exactly a natural fit for a cat.
Until you consider the blinking lights and all those places to hide.
But this cat finds toys more disturbing than cute.